AWAKENING

BY.
ERIC GARDNER

A Thirteenth Legion Series Novel

Awakening
Copyright © 2016 Eric Gardner

All rights reserved. No part of this book may be used or reproduced by any means, graphic, electronic, or mechanical, including photocopying, recording, taping or by any information storage retrieval system without the written permission of the publisher except in case of brief quotations embodied in critical articles and reviews.

This is a work of fiction. All of the characters, names, incidents, organizations, and dialogue in this novel are either the products of the author's imagination or are used fictitiously.

ISBN-13: 978-1537704029
ISBN-10: 1537704028

All quotations from existing biblical works come from Holy Bible NIV (New International Version.) Quotations from The Book of Enoch originate from R.H. Charles' translation.

Author Photo Taken by Heidi Schranz

For my daughters, Victoria and Olivia.

Always remember that those things, which go bump in the night, are real. However the evil that hides in the darkness cannot touch you if you are in the light. Always know that you are protected. I love you both!

This is a work of fiction...

Acknowledgments

For all those who continue to believe in this work;
thank you so very much!

What if your understanding of the world was misleading? What if your beliefs had been manipulated? Not out of malice, but out of the need for humanity to have free will. If mankind truly understood what lurked in the darkness, all of the souls of the earth would flock to a savior; but is that a true measure of faith? Throughout the ages, the Morning Star has woven a nearly impenetrable web of lies and falsehoods. Compounding history's truth is humanity's good intentions to maintain the grand design for how the world see creation. Our eyes have been kept from the truth. For those chosen souls, the secrets of the universe will unravel. The web of the devil will be torn away, and the incomprehensible truth will be revealed. Is your soul marked by the heavens to be among the saints of His legion?

If so, welcome to the Thirteenth Legion.

Welcome to the war!

AWAKENING

Acknowledgments v

A Word to the Reader.. viii

Failure has its Own Cost.. 1

How Deep Does the Rabbit Hole Go?... 6

Our Minds Are Not Always a Safe Place... 12

A Hasty Meeting.. 28

The Dangerous Place is in Your Own Mind 49

Sleep Will Elude Us All 54

What We Hide is What We Value... 57

All is Not Quiet in Suburbia 61

Revelations... 77

Man is Capable of Many Terrible Things—What Atrocities will Transpire if He is Inspired?.. 87

The Beginnings of Lies.. 95

Names are Powerful Weapons 98

The Sins of the Past Can Linger 101

Who are the Gatekeepers of the Abyss?.. 108

Reality Isn't What It Used to Be.. 119

Watch Out for the Things That Go Bump in the Night...................... 133

Nothing in Life is Given for Free. What Price are you Willing to Pay for That Which You Think you Need?.. 141

Knowledge is the Most Intoxicating Freedom and the Most Vile Prison 145

Always Read the Fine Print... 159

A Word to the Reader

"Defiance" showed us Gabriel and his group being manipulated by a secret operative and courted by Heavenly Messengers. Branded a traitor by his own government, our hero finds his family kidnapped and his life destroyed. All for the simple purpose of tasking him to travel to the far side of the globe to bring an unresponsive employee home. Not all, however, is as it seems. Illuminated to a life changing task in the Mountains of Afghanistan, Gabriel along with Othia (an archeologist) and Samantha (a college student) are running for their lives, trying to reach a remote location in the wilderness of North America. The Trio's ignorance of the war in Heaven is torn away as they see that there are really things lurking in the darkness, and this revelation carries a heavy burden.

Jennifer and her two children are still in the clutches of her kidnappers. Manipulated by a lifelong friend, she is fooled into trusting her captors. Ushered to a country house called the "Estate" she waits there in a state of limbo in hopes that Gabriel's return is right around the corner.

The flip side of the coin is the group The Assembled. Headed by Uther Jander, the organization's ill-begotten touch is upon every power structure on the globe. Seconded by Cincaid, whose own actions of blackmail, slander and kidnapping are the means in which she plans to ensure Gabriel will do their bidding.

Our story begins where we left our heroes and villains. Gabriel and his band have just escaped the Frankfurt Airport in Germany running for their lives, while Cincaid and her minions try to tighten the preverbal noose to ensure Gabriel does exactly as he is told.

Chapter 1
Failure has its Own Cost

Power comes at a price.
~ Gospel of Babel 7:89

Location: Virginia, United States

There was a certain air of over confidence in government groups, which existed outside the scrutiny of the pencil pushers of the federal oversight agencies. A lack of humility seemed to course thorough the air due to operating budgets never being cut and a day's work yielding strategic results. Red Horse was a Department of Defense Organization, which operated off the grid. All missions were sanctioned, however none of it was documented where the American people could see. Externally the *Red Horse* building appeared ordinary, mundane; inside however it was an entirely different matter. Linked to each of the known intelligence agencies operating within the government, the office space was a nexus for covert actions. They were not an independent entity, but rather an organization, which could act upon any perceived threat without the legislative red tape of needing to brief the Commander and Chief. It was an organization which The Assembled helped create and utilized to its utmost potential. Within the walls of this agency, and other groups like it, the puppet masters of humanity ensured the world was controlled, manipulated and saved from itself.

Today was not a typical day however. With the world to watch and influence, a single target was the organizations focus. Orders flew between offices, as analysts and operatives alike tried to narrow down where the target could be. This level of intensity hadn't been seen since September 12, 2001. Every system, source and potential lead was explored to try and find a fugitive terrorist. Gabriel Willis was on the run, and Red Horse was tasked to find him. As intellects and emotions ran high, no one noticed the woman walking briskly toward the command offices. Credentialed and intense, the facilities armed sentries did their best to expedite her transition through security. Moving as though she belonged there, none within the building paid her any mind until she entered the command suite.

The receptionist locked eyes with Cincaid as she pulled open the heavy door in one fluid motion. It was something the woman behind the desk regretted immediately. Like a deer caught staring into the headlights of an oncoming truck she couldn't look away. A perfect blend of poise, posture, and power, Cincaid stopped at the receptionist desk, her voice was soft yet her tone left little doubt in what she wanted, "Deputy Commander Phillips, please. It is an urgent matter."

Nodding, the receptionist ushered her through two doorways, which looked as though they belonged in a bank vault. Once inside the heart of the command suite Cincaid dismissed the woman who departed quickly without comment. There was a streamlined elegance to the open air offices, three solid oak desks sat in the room. Only the center one was occupied.

Cincaid had interrupted a meeting between Colonel Phillips and the Command Group Executive Officer. He dismissed the junior officer quickly and soon stood alone with Cincaid. "This is an unexpected surprise, how may I be of assistance, my Mistress?"

The former greeting still held a glimmer of annoyance in its tone. A fact not lost on Cincaid. She ignored his annoyance, pulling a curved blade from the depths of her coat sleeve. There was a misconception about the military. Many Americans believed soldiers walked around all day, every day, with gun in hand searching for some arbitrary hill to conquer. The truth was that office work for soldiers was very similar to that of their civilian counterparts. That being the case, Cincaid held the only weapon in the room. Tapping the blade tip on the desk, she inclined her head towards the phone, "Call in Commander Miller, there are matters he needs to be read in on."

There was a glimmer of surprise on the Deputy Commander's face. As with all elements to the organization, only the top knew all the players. Colonel Phillips assumed he was the only member of the Assembled working within Red Horse. It was a mistake he wouldn't live to regret. Complying with her orders, the call was placed and Miller was on his way.

"You may use this time to give me an update," Cincaid stood silent as Phillips rifled through a laundry list of explanations to the current state of their failed mission. Mr. Willis was now unequivocally on the run, and as near as their sources could tell just vanished into the European countryside.

A knock stopped Phillips cold during his exhaustive rehashing of the last 12 hours. Red Horse was a Joint Command with members of all five branches of service operating in the building. Commander Miller, a Navy officer was next in the lines of succession should anything happen to Phillips during the prosecution of his duties. Fortunate for all parties involved, Miller had been enlightened by the Assembled three years earlier.

In a moment of clarity Colonel Phillips understood why Miller had been called in. Looking directly at Cincaid he continued to say how his efforts could rectify the situation. "There is no doubt that we have made some minor errors with the execution of this mission, but we are rectifying that as we speak. I have confidence in my team, we will find Gabriel within a few hours. The Assembled still needs my talents."

Shaking her head, Cincaid sighed. This was what always happens when self-proclaimed important men were found lacking. One day she would meet a man who accepted the world around him and when it was time to go that would be the end. Colonel Phillips was not so strong of character.

He had been an asset at one time, so she owed him a final word of peace, "This is your last mission Mr. Phillips. Your personal failures have placed decades of work at risk." Cincaid heard the click of a lock behind her. She didn't need to turn to know it was Commander Miller locking the door. Still looking at Colonel Phillips she spoke again. "I'm sorry I lied to you. I won't make the same mistake again."

The blade movement was a blur. A soft wet gurgle was Phillips' reply as he staggered back, falling into his chair. A spattering of dark red fluid landed on Cincaid's shirt. Blood bubbled and poured from the gash in his throat. It took fifty-eight seconds for Colonel Phillips to pass and Cincaid stood staring into his eyes for each one. As the previous Deputy Commander's last breath left, she turned to focus all her attention toward Miller. "Get a team in to clean that up. Consider yourself promoted, if you run into issues you know the protocols to activate. She began to scroll through the new intelligence messages coming in. Miller made the arrangement and then cleared his throat interrupting Cincaid's train of thought and drawing her gaze to him again.

Uncomfortable he spoke, "Mistress, so I may avoid his fate, may I ask what you meant by lying to him?"

Cincaid looked back to the lifeless form still propped in the chair. "I told him when he joined the ranks that I would kill him last. At least his wife and family have the day off. Maybe they did something fun today while he was at work. It is Saturday after all." She laughed at her own poor joke. Then she looked at Miller again, "Understand this, should they leave Europe and make it back to the United States you need not concern yourself with the problem any longer. However know that I will feed you and your family's souls to whatever foul thing I will have to conjure to fix your failures. Is that enough of an understanding for you not to make the same mistakes?"

Miller nodded quickly and was thankful for a knock on the door announcing the disposal teams arrival. Refocusing her attention back to the intelligence reports she allowed the team to clean up and dispose of the dead weight. The smell of copper soon faded to Pine Sol and then it was as though nothing had happened. Not finding what she wanted, Cincaid stood and walked towards the exit to the command suite. Not sparing Commander Miller a second glance, she simply left him with a simple warning. "If you do not perform, our next meeting will be far more unpleasant than this was." The echo of heels hitting tile was the only sound for moments after her departure.

Chapter 2
How Deep Does the Rabbit Hole Go?

Look into the darkness to find the secrets hidden from plain sight.
~ Gospel of Babel 7:89

Location: Germany

Samantha watched in silence as her newly acquired friends argued while they looked for another car. The man she now knew as Gabriel was committed to leaving and making his way back to the United States. She didn't have all the details, but something was wrong with his family. The woman was quite frank with him and stopped him cold in his tracks as he tried to storm off.

"You are wanted by the government for treason, remember? At least, that is what you told me. What makes you think you are going to be able to walk back in? They used you, Gabriel. Get past it, and let's think of a way to capitalize on the situation. We need a car now, and in case you missed it, you are now wanted here as well."

Gabriel stood motionless and simply flexed his hands into tight fists. Othia hung her head for a moment. "Look, let's just find our way back to the United States together. That much we can agree on. Your family is there, and that is where they want us to go, right? So let's at least agree on that, okay?"

He responded through clenched teeth, "Fine. But let's think about this: the longer we keep running, the more chance we have of someone getting hurt." He held up his hand as Othia started to argue back. "Yeah, I know, 'we have angels watching over us,' right? Well, I was there as well, and they didn't say anything about taking care of us, remember? I mean... look at us; we have even managed to bring someone else into our messed-up situation.

"Samantha, you're what? Nineteen?" Samantha, who was actually twenty-two, was about to correct him, but Gabriel continued unabated. "Come on, Othia. She has her whole life ahead of her, and now she is wanted by the cops. Maybe we should turn ourselves in and come clean before this turns nasty."

"And what, pray tell, are you going to say?" Her tone was rising, and Samantha took an involuntary step back. "I don't think they are going to accept the *divine intervention card* on this one, Gabriel. In fact, that will most likely get you locked away faster than arguing your innocence in court for all the false accusations they have against you.

"Like it or not, this is the only way. Maybe Samantha was supposed to run into us. Maybe this is all part of the plan. I don't know. All I do know is that we need to get moving."

"Oh come on, how convenient of a plan is that? She finds us in the airport. Two out of thirty thousand? I want *those* odds at the track. And then I get shot. We barely escape. And that nice bit you mentioned, that now even more people are after us? Yeah, we're on the winning team here. You're off your rocker if you think some divine presence is watching over us. More likely, they are trying to make us fail."

Othia looked sternly at Gabriel. "Listen to yourself. You saw everything I did. You know how narrowly we made it out of there. Do you really think you're that good?" The question hung in the air for a moment and Othia fought to find the right words to explain everything as clearly as she felt it inside her.

Gabriel threw his hands up in the air. "Well, I'm all ears, princess! How is God going to get us out of this? Oh, that's right! He works in *mysterious* ways. Let's cut the proverbial bullshit!"

"Yes, we need to get to the States. After that, you better watch how you hold that gun."

Othia rolled her eyes. She wanted to throw the pistol at him; there weren't any more bullets in it anyway. But she knew they were supposed to do this together, and continuing to agitate Gabriel was only going to exacerbate things.

Locating and acquiring another car was easy, but it wasn't any more robust than their first. They had not gone unnoticed either. Local residents saw them steal the car, and Othia saw several of them make calls on their cell phones. She could only assume that it was the polizei. She had been right, and only moments after they had pulled onto the main local artery, a pair of polizei cars came up behind them. Gabriel shook his head and pushed the engine of their new car harder.

They raced down the center of the three-lane stretch and weaved in and out of cars in an almost futile attempt to lose the polizei.

"Any more bullets in that gun?" Gabriel looked into the rearview mirror and saw Othia shake her head. Of course, he had given the gun to Othia while hot-wiring the car in the airport and had stayed on course since she had displayed the will to use it in Afghanistan. The irony that he had been held to the course to get to the United States by a gun with no bullets was slightly humorous to him. He passed her a magazine, "See if you can get them to back off a little."

Othia emptied the entire magazine rapidly. The two polizei cars fell back slightly. Gabriel heard the slide on the pistol lock back, and he quickly passed the last magazine back to Othia. "Make it last—" he tried to say, but Othia was already firing. He yelled above the noise to get her attention, "I said make it last. How many rounds do you have left?"

"Three rounds. Did you say this was the last one?"

Gabriel nodded his head. This was going to be hard. He looked in the rearview mirror and saw the wide and fearful eyes of Samantha darting back and forth. He had seen frantic eyes like that before. New soldiers experiencing the stressors of combat often had the same wild look before their bodies and minds shut down. He needed to get her focused on something else or she was going to become a liability.

"Okay, here we go. I am going to get off here. Samantha, get the map from the backseat there and tell me where we are. You get to navigate. Othia, you look for a truck that can block the road if we blow its tires." Gabriel saw both women jump into action, and within moments Samantha had their location plotted and was giving him turn by turn directions. *Man, is she good. Her accent is really thick. I'll have to ask her where she is from.* Gabriel thought to himself. Gabriel's ears monitored the whine of the engine immediately noticing as it began to lose power.

"We need to lose these guys quick. The car is starting to do some pretty funky stuff up here and—" The remainder of his words were lost as the trunk crumpled and rear window shattered. Piercing screams and a stream of profanity filled the car. Each so caught up in their assigned task they missed the polizei so close to them. The car fishtailed dangerously from side to side as Gabriel struggled to regain control. The polizei car that had struck them from behind pulled back a little in apparent frustration that the maneuver had not worked to stop the high-speed chase.

The car whined again as Gabriel demanded even more power from the overworked engine. The secondary road they were now traveling on narrowed up ahead, construction pushed all traffic over to the right lane. Gabriel spotted their one shot at getting out of this ever-worsening situation.

"Othia, look up ahead. The truck slowing down, you got it?" He couldn't risk a look behind and raced past the slowing cars. The police vehicles didn't fall back, but kept their speed constant.

Samantha felt the car slump to the right as one of the tires blew out following a single shot from one of the squad cars behind her. The strain on Gabriel's face told her that everything was not going well and that this was going to be close. She watched as Othia leaned out the passenger-side rear window with the pistol and aimed it at the front tires of the truck that was fast approaching. Noisy gunfire filled the small compartment of the sedan, and Gabriel hugged the construction barriers tighter as he saw two of Othia's bullets strike true. The car shuddered as the bumper tore free when the truck Othia had fired at suddenly turned left and struck the rear of their car as it barely squeezed past. Samantha turned around quickly to see the four police cars behind them smash into the cab of the truck and then into one another. The screams of dying sirens and the protest of colliding metal was quickly left behind them as Gabriel continued on their way, weaving in and out of traffic as he pushed the vehicle to make as much distance as possible before the polizei could clear the road.

* * * *

The trio found refuge in an abandoned house on the side of a nearly deserted road. Sore muscles and bruised bones forced them to move slowly into their crumbling hideout. Gabriel kept their situation in perspective, none of them were seriously hurt, and it looked like they could lay low for a few hours and not be any worse for wear. As they all lay on the rotting wooden floor of the dilapidated structure and melted into unconsciousness, the police chase became a distant memory. They had pushed the destroyed car into the small crop of trees some three hundred yards from the structure and decided the concealment job would have to do.

Gabriel had only slept twice since the events in the desert had sent him on this new course. Each time he had awoken unrested and confused. He recalled something being stated in the underground chamber about the sword teaching him while he slept, however, the last two nights he had seen nothing but a blinding white light, and even though it had only been a dream, he awoke with terrible eye strain, as if he had been staring into the sun.

The supposed gifts he had received always lingered in the back of his mind. He admitted to himself that he never really noticed the amulet and sword. He could feel them if he focused on them, but they seemed to stay back in his mind and never really pushed to the front. The items had an uncanny knack for avoiding his thoughts. The sword was strapped to his back, but he never felt it when he sat in a chair or when he moved, even when he ran through the airport. The amulet rested against his skin, but if he ignored either of them for a period of time he could forget they were even there. He didn't even know why he still carried either of the items he found in the temple: something inside him simply wouldn't let them go.

Chapter 3
Our Minds Are Not Always a Safe Place

Blood stained hands can never be washed clean.
~ Gospel of Babel 3:8

Location: The Pit

His slumber this time was different. He found himself standing on a desolate plain. His eyes adjusted as best they could through the ever-present dust and grime that seemed to saturate the air. His lungs suffered a constant burning sensation, and the simplest of movements caused pins and needles to shoot through his body. Fear gripped his stomach and limbs as he tried to gain some sort of reference point to get a sense of bearing. Gabriel paused for a moment and then mentally chastised himself; this had to be a dream. It was his dream, and he was running it. What did he have to be afraid of? The last bad dream he'd had was when he was twelve, and now he was too mature to let his subconscious control things.

The air left his lungs rapidly as something slammed into his chest. Gabriel had a brief feeling of weightlessness before gravity caught hold of his body and brought it begrudgingly to the ground. His hands instinctively closed around the sword's hilt, and as he pulled himself to his feet, it nearly leapt into his hand and began to hum. His vision shifted, similar to a mirage shifting on the desert sands, and something was coming into view. The hilt of the sword heated up and hummed louder. In the back of his mind, he felt something pulling at him.

As the blurriness cleared, a monstrously huge figure took shape before him. It had the basic structure of a man, but the right side of its body and head were animalistic while the left was made from some sort of strange creatures that he couldn't identify. It wasn't from any one specific animal, but a conglomerate of many. The thing looked like some sick watered-down version of Dr. Frankenstein's monster. The thing shifted its weight, and he saw what had knocked the wind out of him. As his eyes rested on the mammoth club the thing had in its mangled, clawed hand, his ears stung as the beast roared and leapt at him. His body reacted on instinct. The sword guided those reflexes, and it yielded deadly results.

The blade became a blur of blood-covered steel as it tore into the flesh of the beast's arms. Gabriel could feel the warm blood of the creature coat his body as chunks of flesh were cut free. The beast bellowed, its voice a mix of rage and pain. It reared back on unsteady legs, and Gabriel saw it take note of the powerful weapon he held in his hands. The creature seemed to finish its evaluation of Gabriel, and as its jaws opened in another guttural roar, it lunged straight for him. Gabriel's sword pulled up sharply of its own accord and lanced straight through one of its grotesque eyes and plunged deeply into its demented brain. The weight of the beast pulled on the sword, and as the creature twitched on the ground, Gabriel tore it free. The open-mouthed stare plastered on his face expressed his astonishment at the events that had just taken place. He whirled toward the sound of applause behind him.

A man wearing robes the color of the red dust that swirled in the air stood there. Gabriel had never seen him before, but he had the distinct impression that they knew one another.

"Quite the first day, huh? The rest don't get any easier, but at least you will know what's coming." The stranger walked calmly toward him and extended his hand.

Gabriel studied him for several moments, taking in his warm features and bald head. His massive physique was similar to the beings he had seen in Afghanistan and didn't unnerve him, but he did hold back his quick tongue, having learned something from his previous experiences. He could feel a commanding presence emanate from this stranger, and he simply waited and let this new arrival act first.

The two stood and regarded one another for a moment, and as Gabriel took the massive man's hand he found his voice. "What are you, the ghost of Christmas past?" Gabriel laughed at his own joke and shook the stranger's hand. Before he could make another comment, the robed man turned away.

"If you would please come with me, Gabriel. I will answer most of the questions you have running through your mind as we walk to another location. My name is Vicaro, and while I can see in your body language that you think we have met before, we most certainly have not."

Gabriel walked briskly to catch up with Vicaro, and he was made painfully aware of his disadvantage in height and strength compared to this new stranger. Gabriel smiled slightly to himself. *I guess it is good that he wants to talk, because it looks as though he could whup my butt.* Gabriel saw Vicaro smile as the thought ran through his mind, and he swore that this new stranger had heard his jibe as though it had been spoken aloud.

"Gabriel, your memory is not as sharp as I would hope. You were told you would meet me and that I would teach you many things in your dreams. Ah, I can see some of the recollection on your face, but the specifics of this dream state are troubling you. Let me be up front: I have waged war for over four thousand years.

I was not the first of the garden's guardians, but I have served as best I can, and plan to serve for many millennia to come."

Gabriel was speechless and completely unprepared for this turn in the conversation.

"Your kind is very troubling sometimes, Gabriel." Vicaro's pace quickened, and Gabriel could see that they were headed toward a giant hole in the ground. "I am here to train you on how to wield the blade you carry and how to command an army set to fight against the worst my kind and your kind can offer."

"How are you in my mind? And what is really going on?" Gabriel finally found his voice, but his new companion was not impressed with his interruption. With frustration clearly expressed on his face, Vicaro stopped and faced Gabriel.

"Listen to what I am saying for a moment. You have been tasked to lead. And while that gift is in you, this will be like nothing you have ever faced before. So, I am here to help you stay alive long enough to make a difference.

"The reality of this place is different from the reality you are used to: pain, fatigue, frustration, and even death are as real here as if you were awake. If you are wounded, your physical body will not suffer any direct effect, but you will always feel a reminder of pain when you are awake. If you should die, however, it will be true on both planes.

"This isn't a dream, Gabriel. Think of it more as you are existing in the pure form of your soul. The actions you take here are still bound by what you call the laws of physics. Your mind restricts the way your body can move and the actions that you take, which is why I am here. This place is a result of our minds merging. To create a location where you can be tested, your consciousness and mine have been intertwined. We are very close to the edge of your reality where all the planes of existence merge. Our presence here has created this environment to allow you to catch a glimpse of what the future may hold, assuming you live long enough to see it.

"First, though, we will begin with the basics of fighting and the differences between your reality and mine." Vicaro paused for a moment, and while Gabriel's mind processed this new data, he allowed him to move several feet ahead of him. Gabriel paused and looked back.

"This is how we will walk into the pit before you. We are not equals, you and I. Never forget that. You are a son of God, created in his image and without equal.

"Those whom you will see inside this structure are not figments of your imagination, but beings allowed to penetrate this plane of existence so others may judge you before they even know you. Also—and pay close attention to this—our enemies know of you already. You can assume that many of their spies are here to gauge what kind of a threat you may become.

"This training, as Abaddon called it, will only occur when you sleep. Your body will rest; however, your mind will be ever active from here on out."

Gabriel smarted at the last comment, truly not sure how to take it. He chose not to question the conviction of his new supposed mentor. He paused for a moment, and Vicaro looked at him expectantly.

"Stop. This is getting too strange. Let me see if I have this correct: you are some sort of glorified warrior sent to train me by those things I saw in the temple in Afghanistan. I have been told that I am going to be some big to-do here in the near future, but now I have to go through some trial to prove what? That I'm worthy? And, of course, on top of that, your enemies are watching. I say that because I don't even truly know what side you're on. So all these things are watching me so they can find my weaknesses?

"Well—while all this sounds really super, and I am sure your dental plan is great—why don't you save us both a lot of trouble

and point me in the direction of Oz so I can ask the wizard
me out of this jacked-up journey and get my family out of danger.
Vicaro's gaze didn't shift during Gabriel's rant, and by his
expression, Gabriel couldn't even be sure that he was listening.

A heavy sigh left Vicaro's slightly parted lips, and he looked toward the ground. Gabriel watched in amazement as in one fluid motion Vicaro pulled an oversized battle-ax from under his robe and walked slowly toward him. "Let me speak plainly, Gabriel, for striking a nerve with my kind is enough to destroy entire cities."

Gabriel saw the blades on the ax glow bright orange as the fury building in Vicaro began to show itself on the weapon's steel.

"I am not here for your amusement or to placate some need you have for a sense of normality. My task here is to train you so that you can survive long enough to accomplish something for God. Though free will is one of the gifts given to your kind, you will come to the realization very quickly there is only one path ahead of you. To put it bluntly, you don't have a say in the matter. You can choose to turn from the Lord, Gabriel; however, those who wish to see your life undone will never stop in their pursuit to devour your soul. And in your current state, you are about as beneficial to us and your family as the fungus festering between your toes."

As the last words left Vicaro's mouth, the ax came swooping down toward Gabriel. The move was so swift that Gabriel almost reacted too late. His sword clashed with Vicaro's glowing ax blade, causing sparks to fly from the thunderous impact.

"If you would like to have enemies on both sides, that is fine, Gabriel. But having a side to fight on is the only way you and your family are going to make it out of this with any chance of survival."

The force behind Vicaro's ax pushed Gabriel to his knees and then to his back. Heat blisters formed on his cheeks and forehead as the rage in Vicaro grew. Gabriel's muscles strained as he fought to keep himself alive for a few moments longer. When out to fail, Vicaro stood up and began to walk [...]s path. Out of breath, Gabriel remained on the [...] seconds, trying to discern what had just [...]ing the questions, turned slightly and stopped. [...] in you, not kill you, Gabriel. But I want you to know that I wasn't trying. The strength my kind possesses is far greater than yours, so you will need to be quicker and better with a blade than the rest of us. We need to press on; we have wasted too much time already."

Gabriel dusted himself off, cautiously slid his blade back into its scabbard, and begrudgingly followed Vicaro.

The slope into the "pit," as Vicaro had called it, was smooth enough to traverse. The hard-packed earth was only at a slight incline, and once Gabriel was out of the swirling red dust, his vision cleared tremendously. Darkness soon surrounded him as his footsteps carried him deeper into the tunnel, farther toward whatever destination was down here for him. He could feel Vicaro falling farther and farther behind him, and as the slight turns in the tunnel guided him deeper into the earth, he was no longer sure his chaperone was following.

A soft light emanated from his back. Gabriel pulled the sword from its sheath and held it before him. The light it gave off allowed him to see about a hundred feet ahead. He glanced back to see Vicaro standing there, closer now than moments ago. The light reflected off his black eyes in the way an animal's eyes shine when struck by the headlights of an automobile.

They walked for what felt like an hour before the ground leveled out. The tunnel was truly an empty abyss. Strange liquid seeped from the walls as they pushed farther into the pit. The sword's light reflected off the shimmering substance, which was the only thing that told Gabriel he was making any progress.

Things were different here. There was no sound, and his nerves frayed more and more with each passing footfall in the silence.

"Where are we going?" He instantly regretted saying anything, as his voice was somehow amplified in the tunnel and echoed up and down the path for several seconds after the question left his mouth. He turned sheepishly toward Vicaro and froze when he noticed that he wasn't there. *How long had he been gone? What was he supposed to do now?* The thoughts swam in his mind for the briefest of moments and then were driven out by a horrifying scream.

It originated from somewhere farther down the path. The cries of pain hung thick in the air and it felt as if they were physically washing over him. The cries of utter misery and torment in each expressive syllable were gut-wrenching. The sounds seemed human, but he couldn't tell. He had never heard anything so violent.

The sword grew warm in his hand, and he slowly walked toward the tortured screams with the blade held in front of him. He stopped short and thought for a moment. *I have two options here: act like the comic relief in a horror film who is investigating a noise in a scary place, or act like the hero and deal with the demon down the hall. Act like the hero, you pansy.* The self-pep talk did little to calm his nerves, but he took a more defensive stance with the sword and walked more deliberately down the tunnel.

His eyes settled on a movement ahead in the middle of the path. A wash of screams, stronger than the first, hit him again, and he noticed a more frenzied response from the mass up ahead. As he got closer, the source of the cries of pain became disturbingly clear. There on the ground, twenty feet in front of him, was the body of something being torn apart by squatting creatures. The light given off by the sword didn't seem to affect the vile abominations, and as another wave of cries slammed into Gabriel, he was pushed into action.

He caught sight of what looked like a human leg thrashing about and screamed for the creatures to stop. As his voice traveled the short distance to the creatures, they stopped in unison and turned toward him. The four creatures looked as though they had been human once, a long time ago. Their bodies creaked and moaned as they shifted what weight still rested on their bones to face Gabriel; their rotting bones and scant clothing waved in a breeze that he couldn't feel. Each stood one after another, and Gabriel paused for a moment in astonishment at how tall the creatures were. They had to slump down or bend over because their unusually long legs prevented them from standing erect in the twelve-foot-tall passageway.

Sword in hand, Gabriel approached cautiously as the creatures left the mutilated remains of whatever or whomever they had been feasting on and awkwardly closed the gap between them. Gabriel felt the sword pull itself to one side, and it surprised him how forceful it was. He watched in astonishment as one of the creatures, who only moments before had been twenty feet away, now stood at arm's length swinging a sharpened bone with rotting flesh upon it. His sword jerked his arms this way and that, fending off blows that were almost too fast to see. Gabriel found his footing and backed away to maximize the reach of the sword's elongated blade.

The ground now seemed to be changing beneath his feet, forcing his legs to shift and compensate—another distraction that had not been there a moment ago. His adversary had no such problem, and he could feel a mounting uneasiness creep into his mind. The familiar pull at the back of his consciousness allowed him to focus on the task at hand. The sword flashed wildly again, but this time Gabriel noted that it wasn't pulling, but instead, it was working with him. Blood pumped wildly in his veins as adrenaline worked its biological magic, and with a newfound vigor, Gabriel went on the offensive.

There was still an absence of noise in the chamber, save for the clashes of Gabriel's sword blade against bone. He spun around and took one of the creatures' heads off with a single blow; his heart nearly skipped a beat with excitement. It was short-lived, however, as pain erupted in his thigh. He looked down and saw that one of the creatures had impaled him to the floor with what looked to be an extraordinarily long human femur. Gabriel saw blackness creep into his vision, and he fought even harder, knowing that he had little time before he blacked out. Gabriel and the blade fused again as his mind slipped, allowing reflex and instinct to take over. The flashes of light and arches of the blade became a blur. He knew he was in control, but he moved too fast for any rational thought to interfere.

Another creature fell as Gabriel cleaved it in half, sending the top half toppling into one of the remaining creatures near it. With two of their number dispatched, the creatures began to back off. The gap widened as they saw something move in the shadows. A brilliant light filled the cavern, and Gabriel cried out in pain as bolts of blinding light coursed through his retinas.

As the dull red of the cavern came back into view, Gabriel saw the source of the light. Vicaro walked calmly toward him. Traces of the light were still fading from his clothing as he approached.

"Well done. Too bad about the leg though. I think we will have to wait to get all the way into the pit and save it for another day. Listen, the pain you feel is real. You can suffer mortal wounds here as you can in your reality, so don't get sloppy. You felt the effects of joining with the blade and how powerful that truly is, so practice. But remember, if you take the sword out of its scabbard in your reality, those forces that you will eventually fight to destroy will begin to hunt you down to preserve their existence."

Gabriel felt heat wash over his body and watched as Vicaro placed both of his hands on his wounded leg that was still fixed to the floor. With a shocked expression, he watched Vicaro pull the bone back through his leg and throw it to the wall. The wound began to close immediately, and he instinctively knew that soon it would be just a dull ache to remind him of the cost of sloppiness.

"We are going to cut this lesson short. Go back and rest, and be ready for tomorrow. It will not be as forgiving as today, but hopefully you will have learned a thing or two by then. Pay attention to the voices in your head, Gabriel. They will lead you onto the path of salvation and the eventual destruction of those that threaten the very fabric of existence."

Gabriel blinked, the question he was about to ask froze in his throat, his eyes focusing on the rotting ceiling of the house they were hiding in. He sat up with a start and saw Othia standing guard over the three of them.

"That must have been some dream. You have been tossing and turning for hours. It's your turn for guard, Gabriel. Whenever you are ready."

Gabriel looked at her for a moment and then a small voice came to fill his mind. *He did say you were going to be tired. No rest for the weary...* Gabriel smiled softly and then stood and rubbed his leg. The dull ache was still there, reassuring him that he wasn't crazy and that what he just went through was all too real.

"I woke up about two hours ago and we were all sleeping. It just felt wrong for no one to stand watch. So, you're next. Samantha looks dead to the world."

Gabriel nodded his head. "Good thinking. It would have been careless of us not to keep a lookout. How many rounds are left?"

"One. So if you need it, make it count." She smiled at the comment, trying to lighten the dark mask that had settled onto his face.

He noticed that she still looked at him with a quizzical look. "Something on your mind, Othia?"

She smiled softly. "I guess if it is that obvious, I should ask, shouldn't I?" He nodded, and she sat cross-legged on the floor. "You are very curious to me, Gabriel. Did you always believe in God?"

Gabriel looked at the ground for several seconds. He shook his head and then paused before looking up. "I did for a large portion of my life, and then some very unpleasant things happened, and I found his so-called grace lacking. So I turned from any path that he wanted me on."

There was a heavy quiet that settled between the two of them. Gabriel looked up and saw an expression on Othia's face that simply told him the rest of the details would be needed to end this conversation. He marveled at how fast they had been able to read one another and how tight the group had become in such a short amount of time. A long sigh left his lips, and he leaned back against the wall.

"I have been very lucky with the family I have. I won't say I am blessed, but I have two wonderful children and a very loving wife. My son and daughter are both healthy, and my wife is as perfect as anyone could hope for. After my daughter was born, we were overjoyed and watched in awe as she began to investigate the world around her. Around her first birthday, my wife and I simply could not wait any longer to have another child in our lives. We didn't have to try too hard, and it seemed as though it was God's will for us to have another child.

"Halfway through the pregnancy, the doctors noticed a series of fatal abnormalities in our son, and we were given very few options. My wife and I talked the options over. All of them were grim: everything from having a hand in his death to standing by after his birth as he tried to breathe and having his lungs explode in his chest because they were not developing correctly. The clincher was the best-case scenario, where if our son did survive the birthing process and he did manage to breathe, he would die an agonizing death as his stomach acids and other bacteria ate him away from the inside, making his few short hours on earth more painful than either my wife or I could imagine. The answer we both came up with—and I believe that any parent would have sided with us—was to end his suffering and to help him enter Heaven before the complications caused him even more pain.

"The procedure was fast, and labor was not quick, but relatively pain-free. Our hearts healed over time, and while he was not there physically, our son Michael would always be with us in our hearts and our memories. The months that followed his birth and death were difficult, and one solitary thought circled my mind: Why did God force me to kill my son? Was he too busy doing other things to take one moment to take away his suffering? Did he really not care? Where was this supposed grace that I had been promised all my life? The shitstorm of negative emotions that followed our son's death was not pleasant, and I didn't feel the hand of the Almighty comforting us—we did it ourselves.

"As you can imagine, or maybe you can't, that kind of thinking can generate some strong feelings of hate. So one day, after trying to determine the reasons for our loss for the hundredth time, I turned away from Him and never looked back. That is, until we had our little run-in with our friends from the other side. I can't say that I forgive Him, but I will say that I believe He exists. And rest assured, I will never eat at His table, no matter what is offered, unless there is a very compelling explanation as to why I was forced to kill my son."

Othia's mouth was hanging open. She had wanted the story behind some of the layers that made up her new friend, but she could have never anticipated this. She looked at Gabriel for a moment and was captivated by his eyes again. They appeared to be holding something back. The striking blue color seemed to want to swirl out of control. She couldn't place her finger on it, but his crystal-clear eyes were hiding something undeniable.

Her eyes softened, and she simply smiled and said, "I assume that your second son was a few years later, when the two of you tried again?" Gabriel nodded his head. "I am sorry, Gabriel. I hope you and Michael can meet up again in Heaven and get to know one another." She could see the tears welling up in his eyes, the light from the moon catching them just right. Thoughts of how he could cope with his family put in harm's way again by God's plan staggered her.

He nodded and looked toward the windowsill. When he looked back, he saw Othia absentmindedly scratching at her neck. "Something bite you?"

Othia looked back up at him. "No, at least I don't think so. I think it's just that the keepsake I wear around my neck is irritating my skin. I am sure it's nothing to worry about."

Gabriel nodded. "I guess we can't really go out to the corner store and get some ointment for that." She shook her head and nearly laughed, but caught herself.

"Well, if you're in the mood for question time, let me ask you a loaded one." Othia nodded and watched Gabriel as he thought about how to articulate his question. "You seem like an intelligent woman. I mean, come on, look at your job. So, being a woman of intelligence, why are you so damn quick to buy into this dog-and-pony show?"

Othia held back her smile as she watched Gabriel try to control his conflicting emotions and make an attempt to sound open to her response. She didn't need any time to think of an answer, but she waited for Gabriel to calm down so that she could explain how she truly felt about the matter without a knee-jerk response from him.

Othia could feel the answer wrapped around her like a warm blanket, offering a sense of security, hope, and peace. All her life she had felt as though something was waiting for her, a task only for her; now that she was on this path, nothing had ever felt more right.

She smiled at Gabriel. "I have a very grounded view of faith. Neither of my parents were well off, and the successes I have enjoyed have been through hard work. Nothing was ever given to my family. As I grew up, I always felt as though something or someone was watching me or guiding me. The discovery in Afghanistan was from one of those guided feelings, and now that I know I wasn't crazy, I will never let that sensation go. My family and my work always seemed to gently focus my attention in a certain direction, and now I know why."

Gabriel sat quietly for a moment, taking in all that Othia had said. He didn't buy it. Well, he didn't doubt that she believed it, but he just couldn't believe they were destined for greatness. His leg throbbed again, and he felt himself nod. Things were very much off the reality scale now, but he did have to admit that he was beginning to find it difficult to cast doubt that they were being steered down a path neither of them was truly ready for.

He looked around the dilapidated house they were in, his arms held out in a mock display of grandeur. "Well, for the saviors of humanity, or whatever we are, we're off to a grand start. Don't take that the wrong way. I know belief is a very powerful thing. I guess we all have our buttons that can be pushed so we fall in line."

Gabriel saw Othia about to respond and returned his gaze back to the window. "Well, I think that is enough sharing for tonight. We can talk again tomorrow. Get some sleep. We are all going to need it."

Gabriel watched Othia nod in agreement and lie down on the floor. He was amazed at how fast she appeared to fall asleep. He let his thoughts wander over how his life was changing drastically and rapidly before him. What was this going to be like for his family, and were they really safe? He felt the sword against his back. He knew the truth: he didn't have any answers for how he was going to explain this crazy story to his wife and kids. But that was for another time.

Gabriel shifted his weight and made himself as comfortable as possible as he stared out over the windowsill that overlooked the road in front of the house. His mind went back to the tunnel and the screams he heard, the creatures he faced, and all the possible futures ahead.

Chapter 4
A Hasty Meeting

What can the human civilization do if only inspired?
~ Gospel of Babel 15:3

Location: Germany

Beams of brilliant light streamed through the windowpanes and holes in the walls, their warmth and radiance begrudgingly awoke the two slumbering fugitives. Gabriel sat in the same position he had for hours and laughed at the groans and blank stares from both women.

"You guys are looking pretty rough. We are going to have to stop for some espresso when we get back on the road." The women looked at one another and smiled, grateful for the distractive image of anything normal Gabriel's words had conjured. Gabriel helped each of them to their feet and then stretched a little himself. He had allowed his mind to wander past hearing his body's complaints about sitting in the same position for hours on end.

Othia looked at both Gabriel and Samantha. "So, got any ideas on how we are going to get out of this? I mean, our faces and names are going to be all over the news by midday."

Gabriel frowned as his mind shifted again to their current predicament. "Okay, look, guys, I don't say this often, so here goes:

I'm sorry. I guess the stress and all has made me the ass of the group, and we have enough problems as it is. We are all in this together, so let's make the best of it, okay?" Both women looked at each other and then nodded.

Gabriel smiled slightly and looked back at Othia. "Do you know people who can get things from point A to point B without going through the most proper channels of certain governments?"

Othia considered his question hard before responding. "Yeah, I know of avenues like the ones you are talking about, and that kind of company I would prefer not to keep. We might find ourselves on the short end of the stick if the authorities are offering more than we are paying these associates of mine." They sat in silence, each contemplating the road ahead.

Samantha abruptly broke the silence, "This is going to sound a little silly, but it works in the movies: why don't we stow away on a ship, and when we are discovered, just pay off the crew and then we can get all the way to...Where are we going again?"

Othia's reaction was blank. She simply shook her head. "I'm sorry, but I don't think that will work either. They would just take our money and throw us overboard—or worse. There has to be another way. What if we check at the private airports and see if there is anyone sympathetic to our cause? Aren't we supposed to be gathering people together anyway?"

"Yeah, but remember, Abaddon said that we should start once we reach the destination in the U.S. But seeing how we don't have any other options and commercial air is out. I'm sorry, Samantha, but I agree with Othia on the ship being a bad place to be if we are cornered. Looks like we are going fishing for a private plane ride."

The three stood and gathered what meager belongings they had brought inside the dilapidated house and moved toward the car. Othia regarded their shell of a car. "How far do you think we can make it in this thing?"

Gabriel shrugged his shoulders. "I don't know. It didn't look this bad last night. Now that the light of day is on it, we are going to stick out like a sore thumb."

"So we are going to steal *another* car?" Samantha's panicked voice cut through the morning air, causing both Othia and Gabriel to pause. Each looked at her and saw the stress from the previous day beginning to take its toll. Her innocent face sported lines of distress. Disheveled at best, she looked about to fall apart, and Gabriel knew they didn't need to be handicapped by more than they already were.

He walked over to her and placed a gentle hand on her shoulder. "Unless we get some divine intervention, we are going to need to borrow someone's car for an extended period of time. I don't like it any more than you do, but we have to keep moving or who knows what group of people will find us."

They all sat in silence for several moments. Each of them knew that the moral objections Samantha had raised should affect them, but they also knew that they would most likely have to compromise many of their principles as a means to the greater end.

Gabriel stood and looked at his two companions. "Okay, how about this? I don't know why I didn't think of it sooner. We will buy the car. I think I have enough to get a clunker off the radar. Let's look for anything that can move and see if the owner might need some extra money.

They walked in single file. If any passersby happened upon them, they would probably think they were a wandering family searching for a place to rest. The afternoon sun warmed their bodies, and they needed to stop every now and then to let their aching muscles adjust to the long trek.

Gabriel massaged his shoulders, alternating back and forth between the agitated muscles. "I am way out of shape. There was a time when this would have been a walk in the park."

"Maybe that is why God gave you the idea to get out of the army, so that when this happened we would all be on the same playing field." Samantha cast her eyes toward the ground not sure how Gabriel would respond to Othia's comment, He refused to banter about the subject and instead kept their pace slow and deliberate as they continued on.

The road signs stated they only had a few more kilometers to go until they reached the center of the next town. Gabriel hoped that he could find some teenage punk or a very old and senile person who would sell their car to an American. He knew it was against the law, to purchase a vehicle outside a commercial dealership required citizenship or at least a local constabulary blessing, but there were few options remaining for the wandering trio.

Othia pulled up next to Gabriel and pointed out a nearby restaurant that seemed to fit the kind of people they were looking for. "Humble and quaint" is how a tour book would have described it. To Gabriel's eyes it looked like a godsend. Chipped paint and two broken shutters told of the many years the small restaurant had been in the town, and the simplistic sign above the door contained a family crest and the word "Schranz," which told them it was a family endeavor.

Gabriel opened the solid wooden door and allowed both Samantha and Othia to go in first. Each walked into the small eatery with downward-cast glances and they found seats in the corner away from the front door. Othia glanced around and smiled. "Well, looks like this place is hopping." Samantha smiled back at her and noticed Gabriel tense as a few more local patrons entered the common room.

Smiling from ear to ear, their waitress walked over and placed three water glasses down on the table, "Yello, I assume dat you do no speak German. Sorry for my English, but I only know little."

Gabriel smiled broadly at her. "No, you speak it wonderfully, and it is much better than my German, I am afraid. Please, could we each have a pint of Pils and your meat platter for the three of us to share." Samantha was about to protest, but the grip Othia placed on her leg told her to keep her comments to herself for now.

The waitress left, and Gabriel held up his hand before Samantha could speak. "It's okay. We all need to drink something to blend in. The meat will give us extra energy, and maybe it will buy us some points with the owner, since those are typically the more expensive dishes."

Samantha smiled and shook her head. "I just wanted a different kind of beer, but since you are buying, I will keep my mouth shut." The three laughed together at the casualness of her comment.

The beer came fast and another chorus of laughter erupted when Samantha took a long swallow of her beer, instantly squishing her face in all sorts of positions as the cellar-temperature liquid slid down her throat. The meal helped with the taste of the drinks, and as the large platter of meat disappeared into their respective stomachs, Gabriel saw his golden ticket walk through the door.

The man looked to be eighty and still appeared to have as much if not more piss and vinegar in him than when he was a man Gabriel's age. When the waitress came for another drink order, Gabriel asked the man's identity. "Boss," was all she said, and it was more than enough.

Othia saw him gauging the man and then she tapped on the table. "Remember, we still have to pay for a plane ride. Don't go blowing all your cash on some rusting-out jalopy."

Gabriel winked at her and stood. Adjusting his clothes so as not to come across as a total vagabond, he calmly walked over to where the elderly man sat staring out the window.

Samantha looked at Othia. "Do you see that?"

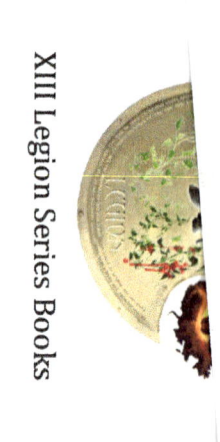

James / Crow,

Thank you again for checking out the series. I know there are a ton of other choices you could have made for your reading pleasure so again *THANK YOU* for taking the time to check out the Legion. I hope the books continue to keep your interest, and if you have any feedback as you go through them I am very happy to receive it. Have a terrific day!

Sincerely,

XIII Legion

XIII Legion Series Books

The question puzzled Othia for a moment and then she shook her head. "See what?"

"The man that Gabriel is going to see is glowing like the two of you were in the airport. Don't look at me like that, how do you think I found you? I just picked two strangers out of the crowd to get into some crazy car chase with?"

Othia had to admit that she had never given it much thought. She had been quick to chalk it up to divine intervention, and with everything happening so fast, she'd never had time to revisit how Samantha had found them.

"I never gave it much thought, only that I was thankful you did. But please, tell me what you see."

"The man and the waitress give off this dim glow, like the two of you do. Yours are brighter, but I can still see theirs. I don't see any of the black smoke on anyone. Those men in the airport who chased us had black smoke on them. But there is something else."

Othia was a little troubled by Samantha's downcast stare, and she placed a gentle hand on her to try and comfort her. All the color was draining out of her face, and it looked as though she had seen a ghost. "What's wrong? You look terrible. Are you feeling okay? You are starting to scare me." Samantha met Othia's concerned gaze and tears began to tumble down her cheeks. "What is it? Please tell me."

Samantha swallowed hard and told her the story of what had happened to her before she left for Germany with hopes of eventually making it to the United States. Othia listened with caring eyes and an honest, understanding expression as Samantha told her about the winged creatures and of the strange thing that had attacked her in the street after she had apparently run it over.

With tears streaming down her face, Samantha leaned in closer to Othia and whispered, "Those creatures are everywhere in here. They are sitting in the shadows, and now I can see them resting on the shoulders of some of these people. I didn't want to say anything to you before because it all sounds so crazy, but if I don't acknowledge it, I think I am going to go insane."

Othia nodded her head. "Listen to me. I want you to look at them and tell me what they do when I grab my bag."

Samantha started to protest as Othia reached for her bag and then regained her composure. She watched out of the corner of her eye, not daring to look the creatures in the face, and waited for something to change. Samantha heard the zipper on Othia's bag and noticed the creatures pause and look at one another. She reached for Othia's arm and squeezed it firmly. Then she heard the zipper slide again, and the creatures seemed to go about their business.

"Sorry, I just wanted to see if it was true about those gifts we received." Samantha looked puzzled and Othia patted her hand. "Gabriel and I had some interesting events happen to us in the deserts of Afghanistan. We just got to know each other on the plane ride to Germany where we met you. There are many things that we still have to discuss, but let me bring you into our shared secrets so that when we do start to talk you will know the history of things."

Samantha forgot about the creatures lurking in the shadows and the unsettling feeling in her stomach that had hit her when they had sat down. Her eyes were glued to Othia, and as the story spun from her lips, images danced in her mind. Samantha's mind somehow took the story it was hearing and made a perfect match of the characters and the landscape, from the man dying on the floor to the amazing arrival of the two angelic generals. She could feel the anticipation Othia had experienced when she had entered the temple's darkness and her elation when the mosaic had changed in the subterranean chamber.

The world had seemingly stopped for the two women, but it started again with a jolt when Gabriel returned to the table. "I don't mean to interrupt, but we need to leave now."

Othia blinked and turned to face Gabriel as if seeing him for the first time. The expression on his face troubled her immediately, and she turned to face Samantha, remembering what she had said was lurking in the shadows. Samantha had understood immediately and was already heading toward the door.

Gabriel grabbed her shirtsleeve and pulled her back. "We are going out through the kitchen before unwanted guests arrive."

They moved quickly, and the two women didn't turn back. Othia looked at Gabriel. "Did you at least get us a car?"

"Later. We don't have much time." The urgency in his voice spurred her feet to move with as much haste as the narrow hallways would allow.

They burst out of the back of the building, and Gabriel sprinted to an incredibly old-looking car. It appeared that it had once been top of the line, but now it was on its last legs before it went to the salvage yard. Samantha heard the sound of keys jingling and the pop of the automatic door locks. The three jumped into the dirty red car and waited as patiently as possible as Gabriel turned the key several times to get the car to start.

Othia wasn't sure, but she could swear she heard some sort of sirens in the background. She glanced at Gabriel and saw the determination etched into his face. It was sirens, and she could feel what else they were bringing. "How did you know?"

"Not now, wait till we are out of here—if we get out of here."

At last the car roared to life, and a large plume of black smoke erupted from the tailpipe. Gabriel checked and noted that the old man had told him the truth: the car had been hard to start and it did indeed have a full tank of gas. Samantha and Othia were thrown forward as Gabriel slammed down the accelerator and the car shot backward out of its nearly permanent parking spot.

The car sped down a small country road and away from the small restaurant. Gabriel smirked. "Sorry. Othia, check under the seat, and Samantha, look in the center of that backseat for a storage compartment. The old man that gave us this car said there would be things in here to help us out."

Othia whistled as she pulled out a small double-barreled sawed-off shotgun. "There is a small box of shells down here too. I thought guns were illegal here?"

"Later, I promise. Samantha, what did you find?"

"A map, a box of bullets, and three polizei windbreakers and badges. Whose car did we take, anyway?"

There was a pause for several seconds as they all listened to the fading screams of the sirens. When they couldn't hear them anymore, Gabriel let out a loud sigh. "Sorry for all that. I have been trying to wrap my head around what just happened, and it is going to blow you guys away when you hear this."

Othia and Samantha both shared a brief glance and then waited as Gabriel relayed what had transpired between him and the old man in the restaurant. "It was the strangest thing. When I was walking toward him, a cool chill ran down my spine. And when I got to where the old man was sitting, he simply looked up at me and said, 'Hello, Gabriel. You're late. Sit down.' Of course, you can imagine my surprise. So I hesitated, and the old man's face grew dark. He said, 'They are coming, and you need to get something from me in a hurry. Next time, don't sleep in so long, and you won't be rushed.' He winked at me and tossed a set of keys. Then he said, 'Red one in the back. Don't bring it back. It is too fast for me now anyway. There are some gifts from like-minded people under the passenger seat and in the middle panel of the back. You're stumped, I know, but listen, get your ass in gear and move. You have about thirty seconds till the authorities get here with some people who aren't really people at all, if you get my meaning.' I was floored. Then he stood, slapped me on my shoulder, and whispered '*Warcrak*' into my ear."

Othia hung her head forward, a look of mild frustration covering her features. "It's an old Angelic word, Gabriel, it means commander. I should have seen this coming. So much for being enlightened! We all need to talk. We need to pool our gifts to make it out of this, but we need to know what assets we have to work with."

"You're right, but let's get to the airfield first and then talk. Can you find it, Samantha, on the map and get us there?"

"Way ahead of you. There is a hard right in about half a kilometer. Take it and then we go about forty-five kilometers, and we are just about there."

The country road was only two lanes, and it looked only big enough for a single car. Gabriel pushed the engine harder and harder on each straightaway, trying to get to the airport without anyone following them.

"Othia, are those rounds that Samantha found good for the pistol?"

"Yep, that is really weird. It was like he knew exactly what we needed." Othia opened the ammunition box to reload the magazines that they had used earlier and found a small note inside the box. "Don't forget to look in the trunk. We packed you a small travel lunch."

Gabriel's eyes grew wide. "What?"

"This note in the ammo box. It says 'Don't forget to look in the trunk.' "

Gabriel slammed on the brakes, causing the car to fishtail back and forth. They ended up in the irrigation ditch on the right-hand side of the road. "Everyone out now!"

The three jumped out of the car and moved off the road. Othia and Samantha stood with puzzled looks on their faces, but the urgency in Gabriel's voice left no doubt that it was a matter of life and death.

"How long have we been driving? Othia! How long?"

"I don't know, about twenty minutes, why?"

Gabriel turned and started to walk on the side of the road toward the airport. "Come on, we need to put some distance between us and that car."

Othia and Samantha looked even more puzzled, and Gabriel sighed. "What you just said to me were a series of code words we used back when I was in the army. We would say that sentence when we had finished planting a listening device or an explosive in an enemy insurgent's car or house. The old man must have thought we wouldn't make it to the airport on the roads and is trying to force us to go on foot. Or maybe they could track the car. In any rate we need to leave it behind now. Our standard operating procedure was thirty minutes, and then boom! We just had to arm it before we left with some sort of signal. Ah...son of a bitch, unlocking the door. That would be enough to..."

Gabriel stopped and turned around to see if they had taken all of their belongings out of the car. "Do we have everyone and everything?" The women looked at their meager belongings and nodded. "Look, this is just a hunch. But even if it is just a listening device, I don't think we should stay in the car. If it is the other modification, I think we should blow it now and get going. I don't think we should leave this here for someone to come by and think they just got lucky with an abandoned car. They are going to see this, so we are going to have to run for a little while."

Before either of them could ask what he was talking about, Gabriel clicked the lock button on the keychain, and the car erupted into a fireball of twisted metal. Each of them stared at the remnants of the car for several seconds, and only when Gabriel pulled each of them by the hand did Othia and Samantha begin to run from the burning wreck.

Footsteps on pavement and then through underbrush, accompanied by heavy breathing, were the only sounds they made. Each was lost in his or her own thoughts about how fast their journey could have come to a halt. They ran as often as they could, walking only to catch their breath. They knew that the polizei would check out the burning car and then look in the nearby areas and towns to see if they could find its occupants. Gabriel estimated they had only about ten to fifteen minutes to get out of the area, but saw no need to share that with the others.

It had been over three hours, and they had not heard anything unusual. The group had made good time, and with each passing moment they were closing on the airport. Gabriel's mind raced through the different scenarios they could face in trying to find a plane that would travel as far as they needed it to. The problematic arrival of the authorities or the mysterious men that Samantha said had smoke around them played out in his mind as well. Each way he worked the situations, everything became chaos in the end.

"Look, only three kilometers to go." Samantha was smiling ear to ear as she read the sign out loud.

Othia smiled too. It was good to hear someone talking; they had been too quiet for too long. She looked over at Gabriel and saw weariness seep farther into the drawn lines of concern on his face. "What is the plan?"

Gabriel stopped and faced her. "I don't really have anything solid, but I have a few ideas. Let's keep moving, though. Look, everything we have been given can help us, but I know that some of the things, while they may get us in the door quicker, are going to make us stand out a whole lot more than we want to."

"You mean the police jackets? I agree they are a little too flashy, but the badges might work to our advantage."

"Let's just keep it simple. We will jump the fence near the hangars and try to find a pilot and plane willing to travel where we need to go. If anyone questions us, we can use the badges. Sound good?"

They all knew time was against them. They had to act fast, be flexible, and pray for a little luck.

Getting to the hangar appeared to be the easy part. There weren't any visible guards, and if they'd still had a car, they could have driven right up to it. The trio kept to the back walls of the hangars, looking at all the pilots and their crews to see if they could find anyone who might be willing to fly them to North America. Samantha looked through each of the hangars for any individuals who put off the same glow that she had observed around Othia and Gabriel.

Gabriel watched his companions' silent conversation; the simple act of Samantha shaking her head propelled them to the next hangar. After two iterations, Gabriel stopped them both with a clearly frustrated look on his face. "Okay, I don't really want to get into this right now, but what are we looking for, Samantha?"

Othia placed a reassuring hand on his shoulder. "Just let her do her thing, and we will explain later."

They had gone through two hangars and looked at over twenty crews. Few had challenged their reasons for being there, and those that did immediately backed away when they were shown the badges. The trio stopped before going into the third hangar. Samantha sighed and pointed at an aircraft that stood out from the rest of the high-profile jets.

Gabriel sighed. "You've got to be kidding! That is a Cessna. I don't know if that thing can make it across town." Gabriel simply looked at the aircraft and shook his head as Othia began to walk toward it.

"Wait!" Samantha grabbed her and looked down. "It's not a guarantee; he just doesn't give off anything. I have seen some people covered in black smoke, but I don't think they saw us. There are some people who have those things on them and a few people that are like the two of you, but they look like people who fill the planes with gas or push them out onto the airfield. This guy doesn't give off anything. He's blank. I guess he is our safest bet. Sorry..."

Othia smiled. "That's good enough for me." Gabriel tried to grab her, but she was already too far into the open hangar, and he would have made a scene.

"Excuse me, sir. Do you speak English?" Othia's voice carried inside the hangar, and a small man turned to face her. He didn't look like much: his overalls were dirty, and it looked as though he had lived for a hundred years. The creases and folds in his skin were well tanned, and he reeked of cigarettes.

"Yes, I speak some English."

Othia smiled and extended her hand in greeting. "Do you know of anyone in the airport here who flies to North America? We are willing to pay, but we don't know who to ask about it."

The man's face darkened, and he shook his head. "Nothing flies that far unless it is jumping from airport to airport, and that's a hard flight for planes this small. Why are you not going through the airport in Frankfurt?"

The question hung in the air for several seconds, and as the man was about to turn away, Gabriel stepped in. "Our friend had her passport stolen, and we are trying to get home after our vacation here. The police at the airport said it would take up to three months to get another one, and we can't wait that long."

The pilot appeared to buy the story and smiled. "Well, I could take you, but it would take a long time, and there would be a lot of stops. Not to mention, it would cost quite a bit of money."

Gabriel smiled. His hands went into his pocket and pulled out a stack of five-hundred-euro bills. "I think this could act as a down payment, and then a sum to match when we reach North America."

The man's eyes almost popped out of his head. "Sounds like you've got yourself a plane. Name is Tim, and if you all would give me what documents you have, I will get all the things in order."

Gabriel's posture changed, and Tim knew what it meant. He shook his head and held up one hand. "Don't worry, I've done this a few times before. I will take care of the paperwork. Go and get something to eat and stretch your legs; the first trip is going to last about six hours. We will leave in about forty-five minutes. I have to put on my extra fuel pods so we can make some of the later legs. Is this all the weight we will be carrying?"

Gabriel nodded.

"Good, see you here in about forty-five minutes then." Tim turned and walked away toward what Gabriel assumed must be an administrative office. His steps were a little lighter, even though he had the weight of several thousand euros in his pockets.

Othia looked at him. "How much did that put us back?"

"Nothing. It was all funded by the people who kidnapped my wife and want you dead, so I guess we are flying on stolen money. I have a few hundred left, so let's get some food and take one last look at the German countryside. We are not missing this flight."

The time went fast, and each of them returned full of bratwursts and beer. When they arrived at the plane, Tim was rushing around in an apparent panic. "Okay, all aboard. We need to go or we will miss our window to take off."

Gabriel helped the two women into the plane and then stopped at the door to talk with Tim. He noticed the two modifications that Tim had made while they had been away; he could only assume that they were extra fuel tanks. "What is going on? Why the rush?"

"Things get complicated when you file false reports with these guys, and if someone sees I have passengers, after I just told the tower I am flying solo, we won't make it off the ground. Now, please get into the plane or you will have to swim home."

Gabriel nodded, and they all crammed into the small seating area in the back. Each took a set of the earplugs that were offered and waited as the final preparations for takeoff were made. As the small plane taxied out of the hangar, Gabriel noticed three cars pulling into the airfield at the far end of the hangar. Three of the men were in some kind of tactical gear, and the rest wore suits. Gabriel motioned for Othia to look, and her face darkened. "This isn't going to end well." The comment was drowned out by the engines.

Tim pulled the aircraft onto the departure airfield and got into position to take off. Gabriel had lost the new arrivals when they entered the runway, and now he wasn't sure where they were. They sat on the runway for several minutes before Tim turned to face the rear of the plane. "We have been ordered to return to the hangar. All flights have been cancelled for the night." His voice was muffled by the roar of the engines, but enough of it had gotten through for the three in the back to know they were about to be put in a very compromising situation.

Tim seemed to take it really well when a pistol appeared in front of his face with hammer cocked and a very determined young woman on the other end. "I think we are going to make our takeoff time, Tim."

Tim didn't miss a beat, "I love a woman who knows what she wants." He turned around and gunned the engine.

Gabriel watched as the cars carrying the new arrivals sped out from behind a building to try to catch the plane before it could gain any altitude. As the aircraft continued to pick up speed, the three cars pulled onto the runway behind them. The dull thud of small-caliber bullets hitting the side and rear of the aircraft inspired

Tim to push the engines harder, and they were pushed back into their seats as Tim pulled back on the stick that hurled the small aircraft into the air.

Gabriel checked quickly to make sure everyone was all right and then turned to face Tim. "I guess we will have to throw in some danger pay with that bonus when we hit the States."

"That you will, but just to cover the damages to the plane. We have a small fuel leak, but we will make the first leg no problem, and I can fix it when we get there, so don't worry. Try to relax; I will let you know if we are in any trouble. And tell your lady friend there, thanks for the inspiration and the most fun I have had in some time."

They all sat in silence for the first leg of the journey. The six hours passed agonizingly slowly, and the small cramped confines of the plane did little to help. Gabriel had guessed it was a kind of Cessna, mostly used for carrying cargo, but it had been modified to do almost any job. "Looks like our friend here is the model Boy Scout—ready for anything."

Othia gave him a courteous laugh and then the three sat in silence again as they had for several hours already. Gabriel knew they were all in their own world, trying to cope with all the changes that had personally happened to each of them. He squeezed up front to talk with Tim and to see how they were progressing. As he pushed his head into the small cockpit, he noticed Tim's map. Through Norway, to Iceland, then Greenland, and finally to Ontario. *Man, this guy is crazy!* Gabriel's thoughts were interrupted when Tim noticed his arrival. Gabriel leaned in, "How much farther on the first leg?"

Tim smirked, "If you all are going to ask how much farther each time we take off, it is going to be a long ride. We have about three more hours to go."

"Do you think we can make that route?"

Tim looked down at the map and nodded, "The last leg is going to be the toughest. It is right at the max fuel I can carry, and the winds will make me burn more than normal. I have never flown farther than Iceland before, so to be honest, your guess is as good as mine. But the math is sound."

Tim's feeble attempt at reassurance did little to quash the uneasy feeling that had seeped into Gabriel's mind, but what other options did they have?

Tim noticed the uneasy expression and looked down at the instruments on the panel directly in front of him. "Look, I did all the modifications on this bird myself. The fuel tanks are unique and a little old, but she is one tough cookie. Not that a childhood prayer or two couldn't come in handy right about now."

Gabriel patted Tim on the shoulder, "I'll see what we can do" as he moved back to the passenger compartment a few feet away. His two companions were looking at Othia's book. Gabriel had wanted to talk about their experiences in the temple in Afghanistan so many times, but it was never right. He assumed Othia and Samantha had had the same idea, and now he agreed. This was as good a time as any.

Samantha was completely engrossed in the story that was unfolding before her. Othia had opened the book she'd been given and allowed the pages to leap to life before her. Othia's story was accentuated by the pages that lay on the table, allowing Samantha to see what Othia had seen. The grandeur was not diminished in any way, but the fear and anxiety of the situation was felt even in the confines of the plane. Emotions ran thick in the small passenger compartment of the cargo plane. Tim fought to keep from veering off course for several minutes. The power that emanated from the book affected everyone in the small confined space.

Samantha didn't utter a single word for nearly an hour, and only four pages had been turned during their discussion. The book appeared to shimmer as Othia retold the events that had led up to the trio's meeting in Germany. Gabriel looked into the book when Othia excitedly told Samantha about how the final mosaic had changed. As he looked over her shoulder, he saw that the image morphed back and forth as it demonstrated the final change. He sat back and allowed his mind to drift as Othia and Samantha discussed the implications of the different mosaics.

Gabriel listened for over two and a half hours. He answered the questions that Othia couldn't when she grew flustered from her mind bouncing back and forth between parts of the story. Then he stretched out on the small seat and tried to fall asleep so that he would be as refreshed as possible when they landed—well, as fresh as his body could be. He tossed and turned for the reminder of the flight, but the restfulness of sleep continued to elude him.

They arrived in Norway without incident and were only on the ground long enough for repairs to be done and to grab a quick bite to eat. The trio finally felt like they could relax, and as they each let their guard down, they noticed how tense their bodies had been for the last seventy-two hours. Samantha shared a small local dessert with Othia, and the two laughed as though they were a couple of schoolgirls walking home from a hard day of academic work. Gabriel thought of his family and wondered if the promises of their safety would be kept and how he could get some proof that they were okay. With each traveler lost in thought or conversation, Tim had to seek them out at the small bistro and round them up for the next leg of their journey. None of them truly wanted to go back into the tight quarters of the plane, but even though they each made mild jests about the cramped conditions, not one of them would have traded their travel arrangements for the world.

They were finally getting to know one another, and Samantha, for one, was overjoyed to hear some of the stories and secrets that she was being told. Gabriel welcomed the distraction from homesickness and his dread of another session in the hell that now occupied his mind every time he even closed his eyes slightly. He listened intently as Samantha retold what she had seen at the fraternity party, the strange man or thing that had attacked her, and the reappearance of the creatures at the restaurant and the airport.

"Well, what do you think?" Samantha sat looking at Gabriel.

He could hear the desire for approval in her voice and the urgent need of reassurance. Gabriel sat quietly for a moment. He wanted to help her as much as he could by saying something helpful or soothing. He shared a brief look with Othia and shrugged his shoulders. "Look, a few days ago, I would have said that this and everything that all of us have been through is... well, crazy. But let's be honest. I don't think any of us can deny that something is happening. I can't say I agree with it, but I won't ignore the giant elephant in the room. I don't know how or why we met, Samantha, but I am very glad that we did. This gift you have can help all of us to avoid the people who are looking to do us serious harm; however, I still don't like the fact we have brought you into this situation. I've got my family to worry about, and Othia is wanted by the same cloak-and-dagger group that has them. And now...Crap! We just added your name to the known associates of a suspected terrorist in the United States."

Samantha looked confused for a moment and then she recalled an earlier argument between Othia and Gabriel. She smiled, her face aglow with sincere thanks for her acceptance into the group and at Gabriel's genuine fear for her safety. "After what has happened to me I don't think I can face this gift alone. I have no idea what the future is going to hold, but I know I am safer here than anywhere else. Can I please stay?"

She felt that she needed to stay. There was really nothing back home for her. No family, only friends. And here she felt accepted, needed, and something back in the deep recesses of her mind told her that she was supposed to be here. The question was completely absurd; after all, where was she going to go? It just felt right to her to ask. And the warm smile returned to her lips when Gabriel nodded his head.

They all shared more of their histories during the subsequent legs of their trip. The climate outdoors became more and more unforgiving as they continued north. With each new destination, Gabriel found himself buying more and more clothing to try and stay warm. With a limited selection to choose from he looked like a vagabond wearing a menagerie of expensive, uncoordinated, cold weather gear. Othia and Samantha, however, blended in effortlessly and only Gabriel was left looking vaguely like an eccentric, wandering tourist. Gabriel grew frustrated at his inability to blend in like the women, he knew full well what kind of tools they would be using to try and find them. Othia wouldn't let him stew on the subject for too long and tried to shift his focus to what was on the horizon.

Gabriel's thoughts were clouded and would only let him look to the next landing area, something kept pulling at the back of his consciousness. He knew it was the need to sleep, but the inevitable bloodshed in his dreams kept pumping adrenaline into his body. He was well into his second day of running on fumes, but his mind was not willing to shut down just yet.

Sleep finally came as they took off on the last leg. The trip from Iceland to Ontario was the longest, and presumably the most dangerous. This threat of danger apparently could not overpower the dull hum of the engines, and Gabriel soon found himself lulled into a deep sleep.

Chapter 5
The Dangerous Place is in Your Own Mind

Seek the teachings of the winged warriors and you shall be damned forever.
~ *Gospel of Babel 3:29*

Location: The Pit/Unknown

The red dust settled at his feet and clung stubbornly to his clothing and hair. Gabriel looked down and saw a single set of footprints. He knew they were his from the last time he had been on the path to the pit. A long tunnel through the red earth stretched out both before and behind him. His mind recalled the dreamlike experience he'd had the last time he had slept. He was near the same location where he had been only a few days before, and his skin crawled. A soft light coming from behind him reminded Gabriel to pull his sword from the scabbard, and the passageway came to life with the light it produced. Gabriel took a few shaky steps forward and saw the body that the creatures had attacked. Small amounts of skin and flesh remained. The creatures had probably come back, even after he had killed some of their group. The fallen bodies of those diseased creatures were missing, and he could only assume they had been taken back to some place deeper within the pit.

Gabriel didn't see Vicaro as much as he felt him. He knew his role in this, and having him nearby curbed the tension that was beginning to build. As Gabriel passed the remains on the ground, his leg throbbed, no doubt having its own recollection of past events. His footfalls didn't make a sound, and there was a small but steady breeze coming from the depths of the darkness. It brought a very unwelcome scent of decay and death. The sword in his hand warmed at the hilt as his senses tried to block the wretched smell. For thirty minutes he walked, semi-crouched and poised for any attack, and then he was forced to straighten and walk normally when his body began to ache. The tunnel finally ended as it opened before him into a vast chamber.

Gabriel paused and tried to let the light from the sword reach the far walls of the irregularly shaped structure. The large chamber was so enormous that it must have taken thousands of years for nature to create, or whatever force governed this place he was in, which meant it had to have been made by something or someone, right? The chamber opening was riddled with stalagmites; he couldn't see the ceiling, so any rock formations up there were a mystery, at least for now.

He pushed farther, and as he neared some of the geological formations in the center of the chamber, he noticed a slow but steady liquid oozing from each stalagmite. He knew better, but his mind screamed that it was blood—*freaking blood* coming from the rock formations in this cursed place! This was getting way out of hand. He turned to try and find Vicaro, but froze mid-turn.

A howl flooded into the chamber, followed by a deep growl. The guttural sounds vibrated in his body, and his mind raced with mental images of what could have made such a noise. None of the images were uplifting by any means, and most were fashioned with the glitz and glamour of Hollywood beasts that he had seen in movies growing up. It unsettled him, and he looked frantically for an open area to distance himself from the creatures growing in his imagination. His steps were sure as he weaved through the rock formations on the ground, not daring to touch any of the foul liquid now covering most of the floor. He couldn't remember if the floor had been covered in the stuff when he entered, and he chastised himself for being too unobservant.

Circling back to the entrance he stood facing the passageway. Gabriel's mind swam, trying to rationalize what was safe and where danger might come from next. *Risk versus reward*, he told himself, and he focused to the front and prayed that the way he had come was secure.

This theorizing was finished all too quickly when Gabriel saw an outline of what had made the noise in the far shadows of the chamber. It was smaller than his imagination had made it out to be, but his heart nearly stopped when he saw another shadow a few feet behind it. His body let out a small sigh of regret as another beast moved in the darkness. Of course, there was more than one. Nothing seemed to fight one-on-one down here, did it?

"So how is this going to go, Vica—" The air left his lungs as he was struck from behind and thrown to the floor. Searing pain flooded into his shoulder, and he felt a warm liquid flow down his back. A muffled cry was all that Gabriel could manage as he tried to regain his footing and face what had struck him while off his guard. He rolled over quickly and sprung up into a crouched position, coming nearly face-to-face with what looked to be a skinned bear.

The beast was misshapen, and its twisted frame was no larger than a Great Dane, but the teeth that spilled out of its mouth told him all too well that this creature was incredibly deadly. A guttural roar came from behind him, and he glanced back to see the other three creatures from the shadows appear. They were all the same. Their pink, hairless bodies shed blood and tissue freely from their joints and the raw wounds on their bodies.

The stench that their collective bodies produced brought bile into Gabriel's mouth, and he had to fight the urge to retch all over the stones at his feet. Vibrations coursed through his arms from the sword, and it flashed out at the beast in front of him. The creature was fast, but its bulk couldn't escape the tip of the blade that caught the side of its deformed muzzle. An anguished cry of pain erupted from the creature's new injury. Its lower jaw hung limp from the sword strike, but that was not the only weapon this creature had. It slashed out at Gabriel with claws that seemed to elongate as they sailed through the air, aiming for his midsection.

He fought to bring the sword up to block the strike and was thrown hard against a rock formation twenty feet away. The other creatures now rushed to get into the action with their wounded companion. Gabriel rolled and ducked several blows that would have torn an arm or leg off had he not already been midway through a roll when they struck the blood-soaked earth. He jumped fluidly to his feet. Blood and some sort of waste coated his body, forcing him to focus more energy on his grip.

The sword flashed out, this time at his command, and the results were better than the first attempt but not as well placed. His blade bit deep into the side of one of the creatures and got stuck for a moment. Searing pain crossed his back, and he was thrown to the side again as one of the creatures' claws dug into his flesh. The force behind the strike had helped tear the blade free, and torrents of blood fell onto the already saturated floor. He noticed that the level of the liquid was nearly up to his shin and seemed to be rising steadily. Making a mental note not to go to ground again, he sloshed onward and looked for a better place to make another stand against the beasts.

They all tried to circle him, but he had backed up against one of the rock formations, and the beasts couldn't get behind him easily. He lashed out again and cleaved off one of the creatures' front legs. As it fell, the other three creatures seemed to lose interest in him and instead attacked their now-crippled companion. The savagery of the attack made him pause. He stood slack-jawed as he watched the deformed creatures battle before him, but when a claw came within a few feet of where he stood, he snapped out of his trance and attacked the three distracted beasts.

He struck at their sore-covered legs first to stop their mobility. His blade tore great chunks of flesh from their twisted bones, causing great bellows of rage from the skinless creatures. The fury of the moment blurred Gabriel's sword strikes, and his mind registered the scene as a chaotic bloodbath intermingled with a small sense of retribution for the countless wounds he had received.

Gabriel turned and left the mutilated bodies where they lay, and his sloshing footsteps carried him deeper into the chamber. His shirt clung to his body. Blood and sweat had coated the fabric, and now it was helping to clot the multiple wounds that covered his torso. Fear and excitement kept him going, and the pain, though intense, fell back to the rear of his mind as he neared the other side of the chamber.

There before him was a massive stone door with intricate artistry. He couldn't read the words on the door—they swam in his mind the way the inscriptions on Abaddon's armor had. The gigantic doors soared into the shadows of the ceiling, and even when he held the sword up as high as he could, the tops of the doors were still lost in the darkness. Gabriel reached for the door to push it open, and he felt an iron grip on his forearm. He instinctively tried to pull away, but Vicaro came into view, and he relaxed slightly.

"This will be for another time. Good work tonight. You fought well, and whether you meant to turn them against themselves or it just happened, it was truly a cunning trick. Othia and Samantha need you, so this session is over. I will take care of your wounds, as I did the other night. And watch out for the lady in black."

Chapter 6
Sleep Will Elude Us All

Are the voices in our head our own; or from something else?
~ Unknown

Location: The Estate, Washington, USA

Jennifer's eyes flew open as her heart pounded in her chest. Sitting up quickly her eyes tried to cut through her sleep filled haze as terror flooded her veins. With each breath the world around her came into focus. She wasn't being hunted, she was in bed. Her children weren't missing, she felt them stir gently beside her. It had been a nightmare. Her husband was still missing, and they were extended guests at a country house, but she was not in immediate danger. She reached for the glass of water on the night stand. Drinking deeply, her reality fell back into place.

It was the same dream she had experienced earlier in the night. Something in the darkness was hunting her; red eyes and claws were all she could ever see. Peter and Marie were missing and she ran from the things, while frantically searching for her kids. She sighed, the mental exertion to keep things normal for her kids was exhausting. Add a lack of sleep to the list and she knew she would be a basket case soon. She took another long draw of water and froze.

A sound caught her attention. Something sliding across the floor. Inching toward the bed, she wiggled to try and peer over the side of the bed. The sight of an antique looking piece of wood with a dirty onyx stone atop it made her heart race again. She couldn't move; she wondered if her mind was playing tricks on her, or had she finally had a nervous breakdown?

Through sheer force of will, she attempted to get her body to move. The voices she had heard had shown her a possible truth to the world around her. Yet she had been told as a kid to stay away from things like Ouija boards. It had seemed like craziness in her youth, but now her father's advice was spot on. A tap now accompanied the rhythmic movement of the stone. As the piece of onyx passed over a specific spot it would rap itself against the wood causing a low thump. With each evolution of the figure eight the knock grew louder. If she didn't do something it would wake up the kids or it would cause the security detail assigned to protect them to investigate. Both options were bad. If she was losing it, tired kids wouldn't help at all. And if the detail thought she was mentally compromised, then they would become overly involved with their day to day activities.

Sliding out of the bed to ensure Peter and Marie remained asleep, Jennifer lowered herself and sat in front of the wooden board. The knocking stopped and as she reached for the stone it halted its perpetual movement. She had no idea what to expect. Her first and only experience with something like this had resulted in a voice in her head. *That wasn't so bad*, she told herself. Yet she still hesitated, her fingers inches from the stone. Soft tendrils of light began to slowly emanate out of the onyx stone. The thin whips wrapped around her fingers beckoning her closer.

She didn't register touching the stone. As the voice entered her mind it startled her, making her stifle her reactionary scream. Jennifer couldn't understand the deep voice at first. Garbled and harried, none of the unseen speaker's words made sense. She concentrated on the voice as a crescendo of animalistic barks and howls erupted around her. Opening her eyes, Jennifer tried to stand up to ensure the violent raging screams were not real but her hands were affixed to the stone. Her breathing became more erratic as she squeezed her eyes shut, silently begging for the tortuous howls to stop. A solitary command, *concentrate*, filled her thoughts. The chaos around her began to move in slow motion, and then froze all together. The deep voice from the night before returned, "Your sanity is safe little one. Be at peace, for your attention will be needed elsewhere soon." For an instant she relaxed, allowing the scream to return. The calming presence of the voice returned as she concentrated on the stone. "The dreams will get worse. The beasts are all around you. To survive you must know their name."

She gave voice to the only questions that seemed to make sense to her, "What name? What is coming? Are we safe?" There was a pause; everything remained frozen as though creation itself had stopped. The voice returned like a rolling thunderclap with a single drawn out word, "Prrrrraaaaayyyyy."

Her body shook as though she had suffered from a slight seizure, as the world began to move again. Her eyes began tear up, forcing her to blink rapidly. Coming into focus she saw a line of letters scratched into her thigh. Her right index finger was covered in her own blood, apparently the instrument responsible for the letters. Hissing as she inspected the wounds, she dabbed it dry. The string of seemingly random letters greeted her gaze, RERUOVED. It didn't made sense, but before she could ponder the implications, a bloody scream came from outside the door to their suite.

Chapter 7
What We Hide is What We Value

That which we keep from each other yet covet ourselves, will spell our doom.
~ *Gospel of Babel 15:99*

Location: Undisclosed, USA

Governments around the world protected information. Whether collected on their own citizens or on foreign states and their agents—data was the new world currency. Like all wealth it was safeguarded. The most volatile or valuable was stored in a series of *Vaults*. Seventy large, subterranean, hardened structures spread around the globe and divided amongst the most powerful nations. These were the nexus points of data. Engineered and sold by The Assembled they ensured that a perpetuation of paranoia existed amongst all humanity. Six *Vaults* separated from the others, were special, kept exclusively for the hidden hands, which steered mankind away from any unplanned disaster. These harnessed the collective information of the other sixty-eight to show all the inner workings of the world.

Cincaid sat deep within the recesses of Vault 665-1. Beneath her an army of state of the art servers governed by a classified AI sifted through mountains of details and seemingly insignificant actions to see what the world governments could not; their weaknesses. Through these gaps, she could cripple or empower.

One Vault located on each continent allowed her to be constantly plugged in and able to ensure her master's wishes were fulfilled. The AI was a powerful tool, but it had its limitations, just as with all machines, it needed to savvy intellect to bring out its full potential.

Seated upon decedent leather, her eyes scanned scrolling reports flashing across her tablet. Each of the twenty documents was an exhaustive report about destabilization efforts. Whether through corporate, political or military action, her lord Uther kept the world's power structure purposefully fluid. Even the superpowers as they are, were kept in a state of turmoil. Never enough to inspire national isolationism, but enough to ensure non-independent action in the global arena. In every way The Assembled were king makers, and Uther was gifted to see the world for what it was. A means to an end.

She was making a calculated risk by laying the ground work to remain within the United States. There were several areas, which needed her skills to motivate those loyal to the cause to finish their tasks. Priorities had shifted, she wanted to closely monitor the Mr. Willis situation as well as be as prepared as possible if the involvement of local law enforcement was necessary to facilitate the kill or capture order. She understood Uther had plans for Gabriel, yet she was uneasy about the father of two's compliance after his flight from the Frankfurt Airport.

It was odd how Gabriel was managing to remain off the grid. There was little doubt that they would be found…but when? The bank of monitors above her flashed with an announcement icon for an incoming video call. She accepted the call knowing the individual on the other side would simply see a blank screen instead of her. "Mistress, we have located the target. I have sent you the estimated route of a private plane, which has been employed to enable their departure from Germany. We are receiving updates on their course though passive means to ensure our interest is not noticed and the target is unaware of our actions.

There is a delay in the reports, however we will provide estimates on their takeoff and landing times. We are planning to deploy teams at all potential landing sites, however at this time there are too many to occupy and still remain undetected. As the list of possibilities narrows we will man each one with intent to capture."

Cincaid sat silent for a moment; Gabriel was very much within their grasp, but small planes made predicting their travel route tricky. Running through all the options, she solidified on a course of action. Turning off the blank screen she returned her gaze back to the screen. The Deputy Commander of Red Horse took an involuntary step back as Cincaid's icy stare lingered on him, "Well done Miller, now we will play the odds. As we narrow the field I want them un-accosted by military looking teams. There will be a medical emergency on the plane after its landing. They will welcome emergency medical staff with open arms and then we take them." The look of unease remained on Commander Miller's face. She continued before he could ask any questions, "The details of the flight route to include both take-off and landing will need to be exact, we wouldn't want to have something happen if they are not on the ground."

Miller nodded and she could see a lingering question in his eyes, "Relax Commander, your team accomplished their mission, have your assets on stand by for retrieval. This needs to be precise, we're not out of the woods yet."

Ending the call she reached into her Tasche at her feet and removed a worn, leather bound book. Two hundred years old, it held solutions to problems the world had long forgotten. Finding the pages she desired, her phone chimed with a message. *Escort arrived, departure helo is ready. All units standing by.* Her next meeting was one she could not miss. Clearing her thoughts she began the complex task to summon forth the cause of the medical emergency she had mentioned to Miller. With the takeoff and landing times, her efforts would secure her master's desires with minimal loss of life. If the estimates were correct.

Eric Gardner

Chapter 8
All is Not Quiet in Suburbia

Surely wickedness burns like a fire; it consumes briers and thorns, it sets the forest thickets ablaze, so that it rolls upward in a column of smoke. By the wrath of the Lord Almighty the land will be scorched and the people will be fuel for the fire; no one will spare his brother. On the right they will devour but still hunger, on the left they will eat but not be satisfied. Each will feed on the flesh of his own offspring
~ Isaiah 9:18-20

Location: Port Angeles, Washington, USA

The night air was crisp as a lone man walked down the suburban street. It was a sleepy neighborhood, like so many in America, tucked away from the harshness of the real world and wrapped in the warmth of private security and the illusion of tranquility. The traveler's steps were heavy as he walked down the center of the blacktop, his brown coat billowing in the rising breeze. He slowly brought his hand to his mouth. His slender fingers caressed his pressed lips. He pulled his fingers away and pointed toward the home as he passed. Its white shutters and two-car garage stood guard over the unfaithful family within, their souls offending to the heavenly host. Their safety was entrusted to the solid construction and state-of-the-art security system. The motion was fluid, and his pace did not falter. His black jeans made no sound, and his boots rhythmically struck the ground in a steady cadence. His eyes looked longingly at the home, in a vague anticipation of things to come.

His eyes watered, and his lips parted as a sentence spilled out softly, "As it was in the beginning, let evils mark be shown. The errors of the few shall be the catalyst for the demise of the many. I'm sorry..." His eyes turned back to the street. Screams erupted from the urban structure as his last footstep passed by the once-quiet home. Horrible cries of pain and anguish echoed across the distance of the street.

Lights came on in every house on each side of the street. They twinkled into existence as though commanded, one after the other. The choir of cries was amplified by a new voice every few seconds. As the traveler reached the end of the block, where in a few hours horrors rarely seen in humanity would be discovered, the chorus of pain reached its peak when all five voices had joined in the song of torment and anguish. Mother, father, son, daughter, and lover, joined in an inhuman symphony that frightened the crowd gathering around the home, causing them to tremble at the sound. Paralyzed with fear, none dared to rush into the home to help, as the pleas for assistance, rescue, and mercy assaulted the ears of souls who had been wrestled from their tranquil existence by this harsh new reality.

Crowded around the home in bathrobes or sleeping attire, some of the neighbors meekly held rakes, shovels and baseball bats. As the cries seemed to move through the home, their collective grips tightened on their makeshift weapons. The crowd stood transfixed as the unremitting screams that had begun at the top floor moved toward the rear of the house, near the guest bedrooms, and then to the front of the house, amplifying as they grew nearer. The pleading wails sounded closer as they moved down the stairs and into the main living room. Sounds of crashing furniture accompanied the cries of pain, and curtains fluttered as if in a mild windstorm.

The piercing wail of a siren shattered the stupor of many of the spectators, awakening them to the unfolding events. As the security sedan screeched to a halt, the crowd parted, allowing its driver a direct pathway to the hellish scene. Whispered voices began to burrow into his mind. Dark corruptive desires reached out from the house, finding another unclean soul to poison. His body shook as the onlookers moved farther away from the car. Tears began to stream down the guard's face. With wide-open eyes he watched his hand move to his holstered sidearm. His fingers wrapped around the weapon, and his breath came fast and hard as it rose to his mouth. The loud crack of the 9 mm round silenced the screams in the home and brought a sudden hush to the chaos in the street.

The night was still. None of the residents of this suburban community moved. All their souls had been rooted into the soil, and not even the recent death of the security guard could move them from the pending horrors that lay within the walls of the home just a few feet away. The eerily silent scene was shattered by the shrieks of twenty police vehicles announcing their presence to all that could hear. Organized chaos erupted around the house.

The newly revealed dank and rotted appearance of the lawn and the decomposition of the house would tell any passerby that there was something wrong; however, the people of this street in the quiet town of Port Angeles were indifferent to it.

The call prompting the police to arrive had come in only twenty-seven hours before. The correlation, conclusions, tasking of forces, and identification of all suspects had been generated and handed down to the mission commander. The report had been linked to a serial pedophile operating in the area, and the manhunt had been brought back to life after going stale despite four years of detailed searching. The news agencies had been notified, and there would be a media circus in half an hour. The hit needed to be fast and thorough. None of the officers had anticipated the entire neighborhood standing outside the target house, but their minds adjusted to the distraction as the operation rapidly unfolded.

The black-uniformed officers moved quickly and quietly into place. Their training helped them ignore the fear pulling at their minds. They would later attribute it to jitters, each missing the sinister implications altogether. Officers in tactical gear silently secured the entrances of the structure and then on command abruptly shattered the stillness of the home's interior, kicking in doors and windows with the surgical precision of a well-oiled machine.

The command element took up position by the local security car. They pulled the officer out and checked for vitals. He was dead, and the officers pushed him off to the side to allow the paramedics to tend to him once they arrived. As officers from several tactical units moved fluidly into the house, the assault on their senses was almost instantaneous. The primary team pressed into the main hallway of the house. They systematically cleared each room, and the smell of rotting flesh was unbearable. The stench of ammonia and bodily fluids washed over the officers as they waded farther into the house.

From outside, the officer in charge watched with eager anticipation. A leather jacket and dress slacks separated him from the tactical unit. He was a seasoned detective, and he was dumbfounded when the pieces fell together for this particular investigation.

Detective Stephen James...this was a case in which he had invested nearly four years of his life. It was his first major assignment, and ultimately became an obsession. His efforts were always lacking. He was always two steps behind as he searched for the clues to apprehend the serial pedophile. The final break came when a witness had taken down the license plate of a black sedan whose driver had been seen trying to pull a seven-year-old girl off a quiet suburban street. The pictures of twelve missing children had haunted his thoughts as he tried for so many years to locate the

Awakening

predator responsible for their abductions. This was going to be the vindication that he and the twelve families had hoped for.

As he watched in unsettled anxiety, several officers rushed outside, their tactical vests wet with perspiration. His stomach turned as he watched them. Their bodies shook as they retched onto the lawn, their bodies rejecting the stench from inside the walls of the house. Fellow officers moved to help their beleaguered comrades, and he felt his imagination race as the information contained in the house tantalized his mind.

"Detective James, they are ready for you. It is not what we expected, sir."

The clear transmission from his radio brought him back to reality. The last comment didn't register as he walked briskly toward the front door, where he was greeted by several other officers who were moving to fresh air after their initial sweeps of the home were completed.

"I need some more lights, and bring in the forensic teams. I don't want to lose the trail if he has gone to ground. I need the area cordoned off, and I need uniforms to start looking in all the local shops within running distance from here so this sick son-of-a-bitch doesn't escape."

The end of his statement fell on deaf ears as his small group moved into the house and all stood aghast at the horrific scene that lay before them.

The smell of rotting flesh was staggering enough, but as they journeyed deeper into the house, each room displayed new evils that none of them could have ever anticipated. The main hall was covered in spray patterns of blood, accompanied by rotting chunks of flesh spaced in intervals on the wall, almost in a distorted attempt to hang them as works of art. The rotting remains of six surgically enhanced breasts stood sentry across from the outstretched fingers of six decomposing hands. The house began to hum with vibrations from a news helicopter.

"They got here fast." The matter-of-fact tone in his voice let the others in his small party know not to comment. Flashes behind him brought his attention from his own world of thought. His eyes narrowed.

"Sir, I am just doing my job here. I have to document this, or we might miss something."

A dismissive wave told the crime-scene photographer to carry on.

The smell pressed on the detective's chest as they probed farther into the twisted pain and misery etched in the very walls of this abomination. He stopped on the stairwell leading to the upper floors and looked back at his small team. The whispered talk of the horrors the team had seen in the entry hall was sinking into his ears.

"I thought this was a serial pedophile, not Manson's house of fun," one of his team whispered.

He agreed, of course, but that didn't matter. This was their mess, and he was the one holding the mop and bucket. His head sagged.

"We need to split up. This will take too long if we keep walking around as if we're in some demented Nancy Drew novel. Call me if you find anything significant, not just something disgusting. This is a hellhole in our backyard; find me something to fix it."

He looked into the determined eyes of the forensic team and fought the urge to continue speaking. He felt the need to calm them, to somehow prep them for what was going to assault their senses, but he decided to just let things run their course.

He turned and walked up the stairs. They creaked under the strain of his determination. The steps looked strong enough, yet they groaned as though they had been witness to hundreds of years of torment.

"Marsh, when was this house built?"

He could hear Detective Marsh clicking away on his iPad.

"Thirteen years ago, boss. To the day, actually. Man, that is a little weird."

The final comment did not reach its intended target because he was now walking up the stairs and taking in all the horror the upper rooms had to offer.

As he reached the top of the stairwell, his eyes glanced at the wall that ran the length of the house, linking all the bedrooms. There was a strange shape made out of bloody remains that seemed to be spackled to the wall. The flies that had gathered on the image distorted it to a degree that made it difficult to really tell what it was. He made a mental note to have the house aired out to allow the flies to vacate the hall.

He walked into the first bedroom at the top of the stairs. James's eyes welled up as the children's toys and brutality of murder mixed in a kaleidoscope of savagery. His memories of his family tried to enter this world, and he pushed them far down into the safety of his mind. Objectiveness came to the forefront. He took in the entrails on the toy chest in the corner and the butchered limbs of a small child that hung on the closet door, and his objectiveness wavered and he turned to walk from the room. The two middle rooms were empty—of carnage, that is. The simplistic middle-class furniture and accessories seemed about to be overwhelmed by the rapid changes that had occurred in the home. Actions and inventories were quick in the two middle bedrooms. He made his way back into the main hall, and the sigil on the wall pulled at him again. He continued down toward the master bedroom, intent on seeing what other officers had called the final resting place of the family. The actions near the bedrooms seemed recent, but the suspects behavioral profile and all the data he had collected, had led him to believe that the suspect would not turn violent. His need for control and domination would cause him to stretch out whatever torture he performed over a long period of time.

He pushed past it mentally, and stood before the closed door of the master bedroom. It was the standard operating procedure of his department to close the door of any room that was particularly disturbing. It was all relative, but considering this house, it gave him great pause to gather himself before entering. He had heard the other officers say that all the bodies were in this room, and the witnesses who gathered outside stated that all the screams that had emanated from the house may have come from the master bedroom at some point. There were no other complete remains in the other rooms, and he had not received any updates from his forensic team, so he could only assume that the reports had been accurate.

As his hand reached for the doorknob, the door heaved as though something large had just crashed into it. His body unconsciously took several steps back from the door. His training had instinctively placed his weapon in his hand, and all the tendons in his body tightened as they waited for something to shatter the pine wood before him. He calmed himself and pressed the button on his radio.

"William, you there? Angie, Matthew, Marsh, Winston?" He didn't try Brad because he was supposed to be in the basement. He laughed at the terror building inside his chest. The uniformed officers had already cleared the house from top to bottom. His hand trembled as he reached for the door again. *Something is not right. Just let it go and get out!* his mind shouted to him, and he pushed the feeling of dread down just as quickly as it had surfaced.

The door shattered from the force he used to kick it in. His weapon trained from left to right as he entered the room. Bile rose quickly into his mouth as the smells and sights of the room assaulted him. His footsteps sloshed on the carpet as he pushed farther into the room. His eyes wanted to remain fixed at the door where the object, or whatever it was that had slammed into it, was supposed to be. All he saw now was blood-soaked carpet. His eyes refused to register the horror before him and parts of his mind were glad.

The king-size bed was tipped over, and its once ornate bedposts had shattered on the floor. Its larger pieces of wood impaled different rotting body parts.

"The amount of blood soaked into the carpet and the number of body parts is too much to have come from only one person." His voice sounded frail and weak in the confines of the room.

He quickly scanned the area behind the door and noticed it was a closet. He knew there was no physical way anyone or anything could have struck the door with the force he had seen earlier, so he dismissed it as mental fatigue. He slowly peeled back the clothes in the closet to see two deformed bodies lying on top of one another. Their broken and shattered limbs were intertwined as though someone wanted them to be the same person. He left the deformed bodies where they lay and turned to face the remainder of the room.

A steady dripping sound came from the corner where the king-size bed should have rested, and he nearly threw up when his eyes glanced on the wall where the headboard rested. Spread-eagle and mounted on the off-white-painted wall was the carcass of a human body. Its sex could not be determined because all the areas where gender-specific parts would reside were nothing but torn chunks of flesh. He shut his eyes for a moment and tried to block out the scene so he could think. There were too many human remains in the room for them to have come from these three people, or even the five that were supposed to have lived here. He closed his eyes again for a moment to clear his head; the images of slaughter remained even though his mind willed them to leave his conscious thought.

His nerves had frayed, and the mind's most primitive fear responses ran uninhibited throughout his body.

"What is your problem, stupid? Everything is over. Stop wasting—" His words froze mid-whisper as the slosh of steps rang in his ears. He shook and tried with all his mental effort to will his eyes open, but they refused to witness the horror his mind and senses told him was slowly approaching.

"Police officer! I am armed, and I will use deadly force. Stay where you are!" The empty threat that left his lips felt even more hollow than he had thought it would. The steps grew closer, and he shook from the adrenaline his body was pumping into his muscles to try and free them from their frozen condition.

Steps, wet, heavy, and calculated, moved to his side and sent a chill racing over him. The hot steaming breath that caressed his neck nearly stopped his heart. He tried to scream, but everything in his body was now frozen in fear. It was as though he were some recently awakened coma patient who knows what is going on around him but doesn't have the mastery of his body to do anything about it.

"*Sahall no zangeloga, mrenta invage.*" The sound of the voice was even worse than the fear that kept him from seeing what was happening. Wet, rank fluid slowly saturated his shirt, and the smell of rotting tissue and sun-baked feces crawled up his nasal passage.

"*Sahall no zangeloga, mrenta invage.*" The voice seemed to come from all around him, pulling at the very fabric of his sanity. "Shall I let you see? The line of Willis dies." The words pushed up his body as though they were a metal pole.

He felt even more exposed than before as he stood perfectly erect as whoever, or now he was beginning to think *whatever*, stood behind him. His mind screamed at him, *Say something, or we are going to die!* No sound escaped his lips as he mouthed a response, but his eyes flew open as though they understood. He instantly wished he had just let the thing behind him kill him. As he stood paralyzed and facing the front of the bedroom, he could see, in one of the only remaining pictures on the walls, a reflection of a truly grotesque thing standing behind him.

Its body looked to be covered in sores and lesions. Where the skin was not rotting, it seemed to be stretched too tightly over the muscle, and broken bones could be seen moving under the skin as it swayed back and forth. The head of the thing looked diseased. Its rotting skin was covered in maggots and the larvae from several different insects that were completely content to feast on the walking compost heap. Hot fingers grabbed his shoulder, and he could feel the larvae and maggots crawl onto his neck as talons cut deep into his shoulder.

"*Sahall no zangeloga, mrenta invage.*"

James felt hot breath fill his ear canal. His heart raced, and fear convulsed his body and stomach, forcing him to retch onto the floor. His vision spiraled, a visual whirlpool of pain and dismemberment. But as the last dry heave bucked him over, the room began to come back into focus.

The floor turned off-white, with only a few pockets of pooled blood. And while the furniture was still disheveled, it was not holding up parts of dismembered bodies. The floor rushed up to meet him as his legs gave out. He caught a small corner chair and righted himself as best he could. On wobbly legs, he risked a glance above the headboard of the bed. Some of the images still remained from his initial inspection. The mutilated body was still there, but this time he noticed a smile on its deformed face. *There is no way that was there before*, he thought to himself. *I would have noticed.*

As his mind began to replay the events that had just transpired, he grabbed the back of the chair for support, making his way out of the room. He forced his legs to respond and went to inspect the closet once more. He tripped on an arm that protruded from under the bottom of the bed. As he lifted the mattress, he saw two bodies, cut and butchered, but not beyond recognition. One was an adult female, and the other was most likely the remains of the body that was displayed in the children's room down the hall.

Something was different, and not just visually. The oppressiveness of the room was gone as well. Some kind of feeling lingered, but it was fading rapidly. He stood and walked toward the closet again. There were two bodies in there. Their rigid forms lay parallel to each other with only their hands clasped together. Multiple knife wounds were visible on their chests.

The radio on his hip blared to life. The loud static nearly caused him to fire his weapon in surprise. "Detective James, this is William. Brad says you need to come down here and see this."

A sigh of relief passed through his clenched jaw. He tried to respond, but his throat seemed to close in on itself. He swallowed hard and pressed the button on his radio. "Yeah, this is one crazy-ass house. I will be there in one second. Have everyone meet me by the stairs to the basement to give me a status report."

He holstered his weapon and walked back down the hallway. He noticed that the flies had cleared away, and the symbol was easier to see. He reached for the small notebook that he kept in his pocket. He wanted to draw the symbol so that he could look into it later. As his fingers flipped through the pages to find an empty one, he stared in dumbfounded amazement at the last page.

There, written in a dull red-brown substance, was the symbol on the wall. He traced it with his finger. The C-shaped symbol with its ends pointing up and down seemed familiar to him, and inside the symbol rested an incomplete triangle. When did he write this in his book? The symbol was covered with flies last time he had looked at it. And why would he have used the substance on the walls? He shook his head to focus, stuffed the notebook back into his pocket, and decided to be done with this part of the house, at least for now.

His mind began to erase the encounter with whatever it was in the bedroom, and, as the mind typically does, it began to rationalize itself as overworked and under-rested.

Grateful for the distraction of an update from the forensic team, he listened intently as they all reported massive amounts of evidence and the large amounts of carnage. He also saw that each of them was holding back something, and they looked as though they had been disturbed to the core of their beings. Brad went last, gagging every time he tried to describe the basement conditions.

Pushing the events upstairs out of his mind, James became frustrated with his officers. The indicators were there, and no one had paid them any attention. Each was so intent on not letting the scene affect them that their powers of perception were being negated. He placed his hand on Brad's shoulder, moved him gently out of the doorway to the basement, and began to walk carefully down the stone steps. His foot slipped, and a firm grip fell onto his forearm to stop him mid-step. The pleading eyes of Brad met his, and he held out a shaking flashlight.

"All the power is out downstairs, sir. You are going to need this."

James took the light. When his forearm was released, fresh pain washed over it. *Old boy has one hell of a grip*, he commented to himself.

The steps were slick with moss and condensation. They seemed to be cut from one solid piece of rock and stretched for twenty or thirty feet at a perilous downward angle. He looked back at his team. "Matthew, I want you to go back to the station and see what is going on. Get the bodies out of here, and check with the medical examiner to see what she can find. I also want you to look into that thing on the wall at the top of the stair near the master bedroom."

Eric Gardner

The remainder of the team went back to their areas. James watched Brad walk out the front door, supposedly to get some air and relax for a few fleeting moments.

Movement down the stairs was slow and arduous. Safe handholds on the walls to help maneuver down the stairs were few and far between. Grabbing in the wrong place resulted in his hands sinking wrist-deep into a sludge-like red paint that covered the walls on both sides. After his episode upstairs, he didn't want to know what the liquid was made of or what was hidden behind its dark-red exterior. His pants were covered in the stuff after multiple iterations of wiping his hands off as he moved farther and farther into the blackness.

The floor leveled out and branched to the left. The stonework seemed to have been worn down by the passing of several thousands of feet. He looked back up the staircase before rounding the wall, staring dumbly as if it were his last chance to escape and vault up the stairs toward the beckoning light of freedom. Stubbornness kept him on his current task. The flashlight penetrated the darkness of the basement, but the vastness of this one room was too great for the light to reach the other side. The room appeared to be circular, and on its walls that he could see were alcoves about four feet tall and three feet wide. The vaulted ceiling made the lower chamber seem monstrous.

He peered into the nearest alcove and recoiled in shock. Lying inside and wrapped in tattered, blood-drenched cloth was what appeared to be the remains of a small body. He hurried to look in the top and bottom alcoves around the room. He stopped after he hit ten and scanned the room again with his flashlight. A sudden urge to finish and get back outside caused him to forego counting the rest.

"This is a catacomb, some sicko's tomb for his victims." His voice carried into the dark shadows of the room and reverberated.

He walked into the center of the room and found three tables covered with surgical instruments. He leaned in, and his eyes widened when he saw that most of them had been recently used. The floor was sticky, like that of a movie theater. His shoes made a sick suction sound as he walked around the table. James didn't dare look down at his feet for fear of what he would see. The smell of human waste was strongest here, along with the smell of burnt meat. The tools on the table were not in order. It looked as though the most recent procedure had been interrupted. James glanced at the floor and saw streaks of blood and bile about two feet across that led toward a set of alcoves. He swallowed hard and slowly walked over to investigate.

The bloody remains of yet another body rested inside. He shone the light on the body, and he jumped in surprise, crashing his head into the top of the alcove. Inhuman screams erupted from the shrouded body as it thrashed around.

James ran to the stairs and shouted toward the open door. "There is a live victim down here! Get me light and paramedics, now!" As he ran back to the victim, he could hear a commotion upstairs that assured him that he had been heard. He slowed and approached the still thrashing form cautiously.

"It's okay. We are here to help you. No one is going to hurt you."

The body had lost some of its energy, and he slowly made his way closer to the edge of the alcove. As he peered inside, the flashlight beam hit the face of the victim, and he quickly turned his head to the side and retched onto the stone floor. The image of the man's face, his flesh stretched over hollow cheeks and the bluish color of his skin, paled in comparison to the empty eye sockets that glared back at him as screams erupted from his deformed mouth again.

Cries of disgust and loud profane comments about the consistency of the walls of the stairwell informed James that the paramedics were only moments away. He glanced back at the stairwell from across the room. His heart needed to see other real people to stop it from pounding inside his chest. He cried out in shock as what remained of one of the victim's legs slammed into his chest. The deformed man thrashed around violently, throwing his body against both sides of the alcove. James reached in and grabbed the shoulders of the wrapped and mutilated body and tried to hold him down. Wails of torment and mistrust assaulted his ears. He almost cried out with joy as a paramedic pulled him out to take his place in the alcove.

He paid little attention to the cries of alarm from the paramedics as they tried to treat the victim. James didn't spare a second glance, mostly for fear of having the image of the mutilated half-alive man burned even more brightly into his mind's eye. He quickly counted the rest of the remains and shone his light onto each face, or at least where the face of every victim should have been. Twenty-six in all, thirteen in each row, all but one dead. As portable lights and a second team of forensic experts made their way down, he instructed them on what he needed and walked back up the stairs and out of the cursed house.

Chapter 9
Revelations

The puzzle's image is only seen when the pieces are connected.
~ Unknown

Location: Port Angeles, Washington, USA

The term "media circus" failed to describe the calamity that ensued in the small town of Port Angeles. The largest networks, LNN and VDC, had been joined by a host of smaller news networks, and all clamored around the home, anxiously awaiting any information on the happenings inside. Other more adventuresome personalities were inclined to interview and speculate with every person in the small neighborhood about the who, what and why of the previous night's events. The tedious work inside the aptly dubbed "house of horrors" was round the clock, and so was the flight schedule of the news helicopters. Detective James had cracked the case, but much to his dismay, he could not have predicted the horrors they had uncovered.

A police officer rounded the front of his car. "Sir, the boss just called, and he said that he is stuck in traffic and needs you to deal with the press until he gets here. All the rules of engagement with questions remain in effect, and since you know all the info, don't give them too much." A sheepish grin washed over the officer's face at the last comment, but the joke was completely lost on James.

"Yeah, tell them forty-five minutes, and I will talk with them." His tone left no room for further discussion as he opened his cell phone and started to dial. The officer got the hint and walked away to pass on the new times to the press.

"Matthew, are you there? Hello?"

"Yeah, I'm here, James. Sorry, I was watching Dana perform the autopsy of Jane Doe number five, and, well, I still can't get used to it." His voice faded away as though he was straining to see something.

"Focus, man. I need some info. Did you find anything out from all the stuff we carted back to the ME's office?"

There was a brief pause. "Yeah, okay. You ready to copy this stuff down? The bodies had been down in that basement, or whatever you want to call it, for about three to five years. At least, that is what she says about the ones she has looked at. There are obviously a few more that are lined up to be examined, but that is the timeframe so far. From her initial exams, all the remains appear to be children, mixed sexes, and ranging from nine to fifteen years old. The victim you discovered still alive appears to be the only adult in the alcoves. Also, they all suffered the same cause of death—dismemberment. The loss of blood was a factor, but they all died off the table, from shock or infection, back in the alcoves after everything was taken off. Each was awake and coherent during the procedures and loaded up with antibiotics intravenously to make them suffer longer."

"What do you mean by 'taken off'?"

"Each set of remains had its tongue, both eyes, all its fingers, and both feet missing. Also, she wants me to pass on to you that all the teeth have been damaged, so a positive identification through dental records will most likely be impossible. This was one gruesome deal, and things just keep getting weirder every time a new body is checked out."

"Such as..."

"Well, half of them seem to have been fed their body parts that were taken off. And there is enough remaining in their stomachs to suggest that it was forced down, not chewed. Also, Angie just called and said they just opened all the drawers in the kids' rooms, and they are filled with bones. All too small to be adults. She is trying to do as much of the reconstruction there as possible, but she is up to nine different sets right now. Oops, one more thing, all the victims from downstairs were worked on by the stuff on those three tables, so the lab is dusting them for prints right now. That about covers it on this end, for less than a twenty-four-hour turnaround."

James hung up the phone without further conversation and walked toward the house. He needed time to think and to get this under control in his head. Too much was going on, and his greatest fear was that too much would pass through him so quickly that he would miss something. The events from yesterday were still fresh in his mind and making things all the more difficult to sort out. His body ached, and his eyes burned from the bright glare of the sun.

"What is going on here? This is a damn madhouse." His tone was for his own reflection, but one of the forensic team members was walking past and paused to get his attention.

"Brad, what can I do for you?" His eyes looked him up and down. "Brad, you look like a car ran over you. What is going on?"

Brad, for all his education, street smarts, and self-absorbed grandstanding, was disheveled, to say the least. The smell of death and body odor emanated from his pores. His bloodshot eyes did not add any assurances to his sanity.

"Sit down, man. Geez, you look—Whoa! I think we need to get you home to take a shower." His smile was missed by the broken man in front of him as he lowered him into the driver's seat of his car. He saw Brad's mouth moving and leaned in to hear his whispered comments.

"I saw... I saw him move into the shadow. He was there, but when I went to look they all reached out for me. I swear, I didn't do anything wrong. I have been a good Christian. Please, don't let him come and..." His voice trailed off as waves of violent spasms racked his body.

James grabbed his shoulders and thrust them toward the back of the seat. Putting all his weight behind him, he called out for help from the paramedics only a few feet away. Men and women rushed to his car and helped him lay Bradley onto the ground.

His body shook violently, and as James watched, the skin on Brad's face and hands began to turn the color of ash and seemed to rot away. The paramedics did little to hide their surprise, and their commotion caught the attention of the press pool that was waiting on the other side of the house. Officers and other emergency personnel rushed to establish a containment circle around the developing scene of pandemonium. Screams erupted from the middle of the circle where three sets of EMTs worked to try and get Brad onto a stretcher and to the hospital. One woman cried out as Brad tore a chunk of flesh from her forearm. Her cries of pain were briefly masked by the fountain of blood that sprayed from her wound. Brad's frantic, animalistic face, now covered in fresh blood, was rapidly replacing the image of the rational human being James knew.

The maddened eyes and inhuman screams did not belong to the man who only moments ago had sat in his car and told him about someone he had followed earlier in the day. James ran over to the paramedic who was trying to wash out the wound she had suffered. As water washed away the rising pool of blood on her arm, James got a good look at the amount of flesh that had left her body.

"I didn't know a man could do that." Her voice strained to hold back tears of pain and shock. He helped her sit down and pulled at one of the EMTs who was not actively restraining Bradley to help her leave the scene and get to the hospital.

The five EMTs held firmly to the gurney that held the restrained form of Bradley in place. Their arms strained to keep it level as Bradley thrashed wildly under the white sheet. As he closed the ambulance door, he watched helplessly as Bradley continued to scream and thrash about frantically. The siren and flashing lights spread the sea of humanity that had gathered around the crime scene, and James allowed his attention to focus back on the house.

"I need to get one more look around before I talk with the press about this." He replayed the scene in his head and walked into the oppressive walls of the house again.

His footfalls alerted the technicians that he was coming down the stairs to the basement. Their sunken eyes greeted his uneasy expression with perfect understanding. This place was poison, and they all needed to leave as quickly as possible. His eyes looked over the entry hall again with the new knowledge of some of the horrors that had transpired where he stood. Distant screams reached his ears, and he knew that his imagination was now working overtime to bring to life the atrocities that had happened to so many children at the hands of this sick individual.

Footsteps on the stairs pulled him from his mental reenactment, and he focused on one of the patrol officers who approached him.

"Sir, there is a call for you at the command post. It's from dispatch. They say they have a lead in your case." The patrol officer looked uncomfortable being in the house.

And why shouldn't he? James thought. "I got it, thanks." He moved quickly, taking one last look at the work under way before heading back to the set of cars that formed a barrier on the street.

James picked up the black portable telephone and strained to hear the voice on the other end. "Speak up, damn it! I can't hear anything!"

"Sorry, it's Matthew again. Listen, Dana is saying all the victims have a similar mark cut into them. The lacerations are not consistent, but it is always a deep cut to the bone. It's that symbol outside the master bedroom that you cataloged. She says it was most likely the first thing done to each victim."

"Thanks, I got it." James hung up the phone, not wanting to overload his mind with any more details. He needed to jot down some of his mental notes, or he knew something would be overlooked.

His experience upstairs would never make it into those notes. With so much time passing, portions of his mind now thought that it had all been some strange dream anyway. He shook off the feelings and straightened his clothes and smoothed his hair.

"Sinclair, come here."

The closest uniformed officer came jogging over.

"Tell the press pool I will be ready in about thirty seconds. It will be fun to watch them scramble."

Sinclair didn't share his amusement at the disorder that was about to ensue in the press area with the cameras being set up and the jockeying for position. There must have been thirty reporters here, and he was going to be the one to tell them that the feast of information was about to be served. He looked at his notepad and scribbled his notes onto the thick, off-white pages.

James walked to the podium and glanced at the hungry eyes of the reporters before him. God, he hated this part of his rank. With a brief sigh, he glanced down at his notes and then looked directly into the sea of cameras before him.

"Ladies and gentlemen, I am going to read from a set of notes about the crime scene behind me, and I would appreciate no questions until the end. The events that unfolded inside the residence of 328 Wilshire Street were not completely expected by the law enforcement personnel in this county. This case was spearheaded by me and several other detectives in the special cases squad. We originally came to investigate several allegations of child endangerment, child abuse, kidnapping, and pornography at the residence behind me. The latter of the allegations was the reason for the large tactical force that was used.

"The accused was reportedly abusing five to ten children at a time in his home. Warrants were issued for both Ricardo Jameson and his wife, Rena. Upon our arrival at the scene, events transpired at 328 Wilshire that drew the attention of the local community. Officers immediately secured the area and administered medical attention to a local security guard of the neighborhood who had received a gunshot wound to the face. Once the area was secured, a tactical team was sent in to apprehend the suspects. They were met with no resistance and all five persons inside, both suspects and their three children, were found dead. Cause of death is still unknown.

"There was one individual found alive inside the home, who we are assuming is a kidnapped victim. That individual was sent to Saint Mercy Hospital for treatment, and we don't have any new status on the doctor's prognosis for that victim.

"That is what is available for the public. I will answer a few questions; however, I will not discuss specifics about the case or about where the investigation will lead."

The tidal wave of questions poured from the assembled reporters' mouths in an incoherent babble. James held up his hands and quieted the masses. He selected a few of the reporters he had dealt with in the past and entertained a few of their hypothetical questions, but he knew the reporters were getting the hint that he had shared all he was going to, and the anxious waving of hands soon dissipated. He didn't have any further information that could be released without causing a panic.

"Thank you all for your time, and as new developments come out, we will let you know." He turned and walked back to his car. His head was pounding, and the temperature seemed to have dropped sharply, causing a briskness in the air that had not been there the previous evening when they had arrived at the suspects' house. How many times had he played this scenario in his mind? Coordinating the tactical assault, rescuing victims, and parading the criminals in front of the cameras like they used to do in the 1920s. He thought he had anticipated everything, and he had been so utterly wrong.

"Detective James, the chief of detectives is here to see you."

The call from a patrolman brought him back to reality, and James saw his boss walking over to greet him. The chief of detectives was truly a gifted and intelligent man, but he was not the pristine image of the police department, and James knew it. His respect for the man was unparalleled, even with his dark 1970s cop look and the fifty pounds of excess weight. To James, he was the embodiment of what a good cop should be.

"Looked good on the TV, James. We should get you a job with the public relations office. Just kidding! I guess this isn't really a good time for jokes. What have you got for me? And don't hold back; I need to know everything."

James looked at the ground and retold all the events that had taken place, leaving out his personal account of what had taken place in the master bedroom. His boss listened intently and didn't ask a single question. James was happy about that since he didn't feel he could have offered any real answers.

"So where to from here? You have walked through the area, and the grunts can do the analysis. What are we missing?"

James smiled at his boss sheepishly. Along with dressing like an old-school cop, his feelings about finances were old school as well. "I have Matthew working the databases for any matches to any of the details inside. I need freedom of movement on this—no department red tape. The image on the wall near the master bedroom was carved into all the victims they have examined so far. I need to follow that rabbit if it shows up. I am going to leave the team here to relay info to me and keep working the details, but I think we need to get the information firsthand from other agencies."

The frown of his boss's face was expected, but not as set as usual. "As much as I dislike it, you got it. This is some really sick stuff, and you have as much leash as you need, just don't hang yourself with it."

James looked at the house again and felt his boss's hand on his shoulder. "I got this. Why don't you go and check on Brad and head home. You need to get some sleep. Or at least reset your mind. I will wrap things up here."

James turned to protest, but his boss was already walking toward the house, issuing orders and informing everyone within earshot that he was going to be the officer in charge for the remainder of the evidence-collection process and that all questions should go through him and Detective James's forensic team.

James smiled. Outmaneuvered again, oh well. He turned and entered his car and began to dial Matthew at the station.

"Hey, I was just about to call you. We got another scene with your mark on it."

James paused for a moment to collect his thoughts. "Where?"

"It was seen at an armored car hit about four hours from here two days ago. The suspects stole everything inside and killed both the driver and passenger."

"I need transport to the location where the mark has come up, and any preliminary information you can give me. Use whatever we need, and ask for a helicopter rental. The chief gave me permission to keep the heat on the investigation, and I need to head out in the morning. I am going to pack, get some shuteye, and I will be in to the office about five tonight. Also I want you to run a name for me. Willis. Can you have that stuff ready by then?"

"Not a problem. I will gather all the new stuff we got from the crime scene also so you will have the entire picture. Where did the name come from? I haven't seen that in any of the notes."

There was a pause on the other end of the phone, and James cleared his throat. "It is a hunch, I guess, just run it to ground for me. I am going to see Brad on the way home. I will let you know what they say. Don't worry, he will be fine, and I will make sure he is getting everything they can give him to get him better."

"Thanks, let me know if you need anything else."

There was a click, and James put down his cell phone. He knew that Matthew felt guilty about Brad. The two were close, and James knew the kind of thoughts that were running through his mind.

James made a mental note to talk to his entire team when he got back. He would give them some time to work out some of the issues they had on their own, but he wanted to ensure they all talked to each other and possibly to the department psychologist so there were no repeats of Brad's fate in the future.

Chapter 10
Man is Capable of Many Terrible Things—What Atrocities will Transpire if He is Inspired?

Sacrifices for the Morning Star saturated the consecrated ground so completely, his legions could march on the Gates of Heaven unscathed.
~ Gospel of Babel 46:19

Location: Undisclosed, USA

Cincaid stood silent, her back resting against the cool, jagged walls of a subterranean passageway. Her naked frame swallowed by darkness, she waited for the torchlight at the far end of the passageway to make its way toward her. The smell of mildew and damp dirt clung to her body, and she resisted the temptation to warm her skin. Her body stood rigid, allowing the darkness to penetrate into the depths of her being. Her eyes stared blankly, her mind far away, lavishing in the events that would soon transpire.

A shuffling of feet in the distance brought her mind back to the present, and she refocused her eyes to the far end of the passageway. Two hundred feet away, a small flame began to push the darkness back, and in her mind she could picture the long-robed figure walking slowly toward her. She forced her body to remain calm. Her chest tightened in anticipation as new flashes of light came to life, stretching out behind the original flame. Agonizing minutes passed like an ice age until she felt the warmth of the flames finally reach her gooseflesh-covered skin.

As her pupils adjusted to the light, she could see the dark smile of her master from the depths of the familiar black-hooded robe. Cincaid reveled in the lustfulness in his eyes, but she forced her body to remain calm. Everything had to be perfect. She would not be the catalyst for his rage. Too many times in the recent past, the desires of the Assembled had jeopardized the purity of the ceremony and resulted in devastating failure. Images pushed to the forefront of her mind as she recalled the sacrificed multitude of nameless victims required to appease the vile beings they communicated with, each demanding the most appalling bloodshed for failure.

Her eyes focused back on the nefarious smile of her master. The bare flesh of those standing behind him caught her eye, forcing her mental restraint to the maximum. Many in the assembly had commented on the unnatural appeal that Uther possessed during normal meetings; she knew from personal experience that it paled in comparison to when he practiced his dark arts. Those moments stirred a nearly insatiable craving. She fought to bring her desires back under control as he walked past, the soft fabric of his robe caressing her warming skin. She turned and followed directly behind his broad form. The procession paused to allow her to take her rightful place in the unspoken hierarchy among them.

Flickering shadows danced on the walls as the procession walked along. The torches warmed the naked bodies of the gathered members as they ventured farther down the passageway. They walked in utter silence, their footsteps and breathing echoing in the passageway as they progressed into the depths of the darkness before them.

Cincaid's eyes widened as Uther led them into a massive chamber. There had been hundreds of gatherings like this in the past; however, none had ever held such potential for success.

Her pulse quickened as the torches were placed in mounts along the walls, illuminating massive tapestries and heinous icons that had been erected to pay homage to the forgotten beings that slumbered under the fabric of creation. Her eyes rested on one tapestry. It was always the same: each time she entered this sanctuary, her thoughts and eyes always lingered on its dark meaning.

Stretching fifty feet across and as many high, the blood-drenched fibers depicted the unnatural birth of countless demonic creatures. Thirteen cloaked figures stood around hundreds of women, their naked flesh covered in blood as each struggled to hold in the demonic beast that threatened to tear free from inside its horror-stricken host.

She always found the same woman in the sea of tormented faces. Their eyes met each time she came into the sanctuary. They were nearly the same age. The tightness of her skin and the flawlessness of the unnamed woman's features told her everything she needed to know about her age and status in life. The utter terror etched on the woman's face was intoxicating to Cincaid.

To be impregnated by one of the first creations in the universe and to see the knowledge that rested in its ancient eyes moments before her own entrance to oblivion was an experience Cincaid longed for. She knew she would never be one of the chosen: her flesh was already corrupted by man. The offspring of such a union was hinted at in history. Attempts to write them out, erasing them from the minds of man had failed. Conquers always knew the true history and her master had shared their story of destruction with her. Those chosen for the honor of motherhood to carry a descendant of the firstborn were pure of body and innocent of mind. There could be no taint of corruption, and any hint of faith in the false Father or pleasures of the flesh would ruin the vessel.

She shifted her gaze from the bloody scene that she had lovingly caressed with her eyes and walked with bowed head to her place among the Assembled. She stood perfectly still, lifting her head at the predestined time. Once the Assembled were together, each movement was executed precisely.

Uther stood on an elevated platform, his robed body half hidden behind an altar of human bones. The altar's construction had taken three hundred unwilling victims and twelve years to complete. She took particular pride in the centerpiece. Her own hands had crafted the icon that rested in the heart of the altar. Fused human ribs had been made into the letter C, and dried tissue and tendons held a final piece that had been created from a combination of over forty human hand bones. She didn't know its true meaning—only Uther knew those dark secrets—but her heart swelled with pride each time she witnessed him standing behind it while addressing the gathered followers.

Cincaid watched as he looked over the assembled group of forty-five followers. Their naked bodies shimmered with sweat from the heat of the torches placed around the subterranean chamber. Uther lifted his hands up and then out toward the group. With head downcast, he began to softly chant.

Cincaid listened for her cue. She would lend her voice to her master's and then the next in line of succession would join in. It had taken her three years to learn the nuances of this ceremony. The words spoken were not truly words at all, but seemingly animalistic grunts and guttural roars. With each syllable, pain coursed through her body. If she misspoke, the consequences would be disastrous.

Out of the corner of her eye she caught sight of the man standing next to her, his body toned, flawless, and covered in sweat. An incorrect syllable struck like a hammer into her ear canal, and her eyes registered the fountain of blood that erupted from his mouth, shooting skyward. The man shook violently and fell to the floor. No one moved to help him. Each of the Assembled was focused on reciting the syllables correctly.

Three hours passed, and Cincaid felt the fatigue in her body as she fought to maintain her place in the ceremony. There was truly no way of knowing when the ritual would end. The conclusion rested in the hands of Uther.

Cincaid watched as Uther's hands moved crisply through the air. She could see his brow furrow in concentration. Sweat flowed down his face as he concentrated on the ancient book that rested on the altar before him. Every movement, including his facial gestures, was a preplanned orchestration of flawless precision. She had seen him practice this ceremony for hours each day, and ultimately he would be given an unseen sign when the ritual was to end.

The choir of the Assembled rose as each felt a tug in their stomachs that indicated a change in the ritual. The sounds they uttered opened a connection to all those partaking in the event. None of them could explain it, but they all understood its importance.

Cincaid could feel the vibrations of energy that flowed from the stone altar, striking walls and crashing back onto the Assembled. She could feel the ripples of pure power wash over her glistening body as she struggled to raise her voice. Each member present for this ceremony was a favored student of Uther's. Cincaid was special in a way: he never regarded her as a pupil; she always felt as though he perceived her as more of an extension of himself.

The collective voices of the Assembled reached a violent crescendo, which ended with an abrupt silence. Each of them stopped precisely as the last syllable left their mouth.

Uther slowly and silently walked to the passageway where they had all entered. He extended his arm and ushered them to leave. Cincaid was the first to step forward, pausing when she saw a glimmer in his eye. He held up a hand, and she moved behind him and stood silently. Her body, although taxed beyond belief, now felt renewed as a fresh wave of adrenaline flowed through it. Something was different. She had never seen Uther so vibrant after the ritual. She moved behind him and stood silent. Each of the Assembled left in turn, their sweat-covered bodies disappearing into the darkness. Their torches remained in the sconces in which they had been placed, extinguished one by one as their former bearers left the chamber.

Soon only one member remained. Two torches cast their flickering light upon Uther and the woman. She was saturated with sweat, auburn hair flattened upon her head. She stood rigidly waiting for Uther's permission to leave.

Cincaid knew her. She had been one of the Assembled for over a decade. Nearly forty, her body was still firm and attractive. The woman was a fanatic about makeup, and Cincaid could see how the sweat had eaten through the thick layer of foundation that had been applied perfectly just hours before.

Cincaid watched as a shiver crept up the woman's spine, causing her to shake faintly. Smiling, Uther stepped in front of her, blocking her passage. Cincaid took a step forward at Uther's command, and she cast her eyes down respectfully. She felt two points of boiling heat on her chin, and she stifled a cry of pain as she looked up. Uther's fingers were lightly touching her, his skin internally ablaze. She saw a familiar twinkle in his eye as pain-filled tears began to stream down her face. His potent gaze turned back to the last of the Assembled who stood before him.

Like warm milk, Uther's soothing voice calmed the woman as his words caressed her ears. Her body swayed back and forth as though caught in a trance.

"Today we pave the way for our true creators, those who have filled our souls with purpose and prosperity, who have bestowed upon us the knowledge of creation, of the joy of pleasure and the intoxication of war. There is no greater death than to be a sacrifice in their name. Your untouched soul has been chosen. It will excite their palates, awakening a hunger for our unworthy enemies."

Cincaid watched, transfixed. This was all new. Something wonderful was about to be revealed, and she willed her eyes to stay open, fearful that she would miss something should she even blink.

Uther pulled an ancient-looking dagger from the depths of his robe. Its hilt was made of some kind of animal bone. The blade itself was black as night. He held it out in front of the woman before him. Her body still swayed in time with an unheard beat. With one brutal stroke, Uther drove the blade deep into her body, just below the navel, heaving with both hands and pulling it toward her throat.

Gore exploded from the woman's body. Her blood and organs slammed into Uther with such force that he staggered back. In an instant, he regained his footing and stepped back toward the woman, his robe saturated with blood. His right hand quickly caught the woman by the chin as she began to crumple before him. Cincaid could see that the trance had worn off, and the expression of fear and pain was similar to the woman's on the tapestry in the chamber. Cincaid envied her. Uther kissed his victim deeply as her organs continued to spill onto the floor. The embrace ended, and he let go of her chin, allowing her to fall to the floor.

Uther turned to Cincaid, and she saw the lustful gaze that he had worn earlier in the passageway. Her heart beat rapidly, and she felt her skin begin to warm. Sweat mixed with the iron smell of blood swirled in her nose, causing her head to spin. The smell of jasmine lingered in the air as an uncontrollable sexual urge came over her.

She tore at Uther's blood-drenched robes. Within seconds his body was bare. Cincaid's athletic arms and toned legs were now covered in the bloody remains that had covered Uther's robes. Her flat stomach and ample chest were splattered crimson, as though a crazed modern artist had painted a swirling splash of death over her tanned skin.

She stared lustfully at his muscular body. He grinned at her. Not a word was spoken as he laid her down at the entrance of the chamber. She felt his hot breath in her ear.

"We have brought forth the first of two tonight."

She sighed as his burning hands caressed her body. Within moments, the passageway was filled with the sounds of passion as Uther made another appeasement to the firstborn of creation—a blasphemous sin against God.

Chapter 11
The Beginnings of Lies.

The lies of history become the facts of tomorrow.
~ Unknown

Location: Vault 66-1, USA

The smell of copper infused with passion remained at the forefront of Cincaid's senses as she moved into the depths of the *Vault* again. She could still feel Uther's firm hands on her, as she remembered their animalistic encounter. There was nothing she wouldn't do for him, to include ignoring her own pleasures in order to accomplish his wishes. A low murmur of concern was surfacing amongst the upper echelon of the Assembled. Uther needed to remain focused on his efforts so any distraction was unacceptable. Their angst was due to a complication with one of their collection sites.

Power did not come naturally to humanity. Those select few who discovered how to align themselves with it could accomplish anything; though it came at a price. Like anything, the cost was associated with the service. Her master had incalculable ambitions, and thusly, the expense was high.

The collection house was a means to transform the weakness of the flesh into capital. Which Uther could use to entice the darkness itself to bend to his will. There were many sites all around the globe, yet losing even one would be painful. Complicating things further a potent rune of power utilized by the Assembled was surfacing at sites where the group had been active. The implications of a member within their ranks sloppily tagging the locations were impossible. The compartmentalization efforts they employed would have prevented this from occurring. Only a set number of members knew all the details and their loyalty was beyond questioning. This was something else. Clearly something was working to counter their efforts or expose them to the masses. Their place in society would come out in due time, however now would be counterproductive.

Scrolling through the data she pulled up the personnel file of the local police detective who was investigating the discovery of the collection house. Seemingly uncorrupted, Stephen James appeared to be a potential asset. She paused and opened the list of potential local law enforcement agents to use if Mr. Willis surfaced in the area and smiled as she found Mr. James' name was among them. A strange coincidence, or were the powers that be illuminating a person to be brought into the fold? James' courtship was inconsequential since Uther handled recruitment. This was a matter of determining if James would be effective in their cause.

The intelligence regarding Gabriel had gone dry. Even the dark creation she sent was silent, a strange thing, contributed to the power spike in the ethereal realm after Uther's previous ritual. Since her participation in the dark rite all of her other worldly talents were askew. With no new data on Gabriel she would focus her energies on solving this small crisis. Intrigue could inspire, but curiosity could kill. Even a seasoned cop like this James could find his professional will broken if she pulled back the curtain. Give him enough of a view into the darkness to illuminate him to the insignificance of his actions.

With any seekers of truth, it really never mattered what they discovered. It was the very act of searching that fulfilled them. A sprinkling of truth over a superbly manipulated reality was just the thing to thwart Mr. James' efforts. Should his services be needed to take care of Gabriel and his friends then she would simply spin the tales together.

Contingency plans with false intelligence reports from CIA, FBI, and HS were already available for her to steer James away from personally discovering any real information about the Assembled. She would need to craft the data to link Gabriel to the nefarious reports, so in the event James was needed he would be all the more willing to take him down.

It seemed the Mr. Willis was going to get another adversary, and the shadows would still conceal their true purpose. This would please Uther greatly. Cincaid allowed her thoughts to wonder for a moment, envisioning the pleasures she would endure for accomplishing so much for their cause.

Chapter 12
Names are Powerful Weapons

Are the dreams we have windows into the future? Then what are nightmares?
~ Unknown

Location: The Estate, USA

The sun felt incredible on her face, but as it dipped below the trees Jennifer felt a chill run down her back. Calling Peter and Marie over she held them close on her lap. Each of them enjoying the setting sun from the steps of the *Estate*. Her repeated requests to leave were met with countless excuses, so soon it was very apparent she and the kids were not going anywhere. They spent as much time outdoors as possible lately. She told the security guards it was to wear the kids out so they would sleep better. It was a believable lie. The truth was difficult to articulate. The nightmares she suffered from were monstrously terrifying, and any time spent in the house awake felt oppressed. She was even hesitant to blink for fear it would bring back the terrible visions from the night before.

She prayed and concentrated on the stone, and while the voice didn't come back there was a feeling of peace. The cuts in her leg still bewildered her. She carried a small notebook and wrote the string of letters over and over hoping she would see a pattern, perhaps like a vanity license plate, but she could think of nothing.

Peter and Marie still seemed unaffected. According to them, their dreams were filled with playful adventures and talking animals. She envied them to a degree, but vowed to take all the bad dreams if it kept her beautiful angels happy and healthy.

The nights were not kind to the others in the house. It had started as a bizarre accident. One of the security detail had tripped and somehow impaled himself on a tactical knife he carried. It was a grizzly scene, with surprisingly little blood she recalled. He had cut his femoral artery and bled out while they tried to bring help. Jennifer had looked outside her door as the cries for help had flooded the hallway. The man's shocked expression told her he was more surprised than she was about falling on the blade. He had screamed only once then he simply sat as his friends tried to save him, his blood absorbing directly into the floor beneath him.

Now, a new injury occurred nightly. If the security detail were not highly trained professionals the incidents could have been written off as accidents. Or if only a few of the agents had been affected the cuts and bruises could have been seen as self-inflicted. However every member of the team had experienced something unexplainable; well everyone except Agent Times the team leader. Understandably this aided in Jennifer's request to be outside more. They all were aware that no one was accosted out in the open.

Jennifer had overheard two recently injured agents arguing with their superior. Agent Times had dismissed them as delusional and looking for a way to get out from an uneventful mission. He refused their pleas to report the events. Maybe it was a natural gas leak and they were all going crazy slowly. Or perhaps the well on the property had somehow gotten contaminated. The two agents offered a multitude of explanations, each grounded and plausible, and all within the acceptable parameters of seeking guidance. Each was rejected.

The chime from the grandfather clock in the entry way signaled the end of their stay outdoors. The routine had been embedded enough that no one needed prompting to move inside. As soon as they entered the house Marie began begging for a bed time snack. Not surprised, Jennifer agreed and both children shouted for joy.

The short walk to the kitchen had Marie singing several recently invented songs. One caught Jennifer's attention more than the others. Marine was bouncing back and forth between the hallway walls and with each touch she would recite a letter. Studying the alphabet was one of the many games they used to pass the time. Marie would shout "D", then race to the other wall and proclaimed "E". The string was eight letters long.

Puzzled, Jennifer asked, "where does that song come from?"

Marie smiled broadly and tapped the pad of paper Jennifer was carrying. Without skipping a beat, she went into the full chorus, "D-E-V-O-U-R-E-R, D-E-V-O-U-R-E-R, D-E-V-O-U-R-E-R!" Jennifer stared at her daughter in disbelief. She had solved the riddle. The letters had been backward. Yet learning what the letters spelled held its own terror. So that was the name of what was coming, or was that the name of what was already there?

As though the name was the final piece of the puzzle, Jennifer saw all the events for what they were. Whatever the Devourer was and whether it was in the house or not was only a single segment of the larger problem; something was trying to get them.

Out of the corner of her vision Jennifer saw the security agent on the far side of the kitchen fall to the ground. His hands tore at his face while he screamed for someone to get "it" off him. Jennifer pulled Marie and Peter back from the chaotic scene as more agents rushed in to help. In a whispered prayer she said, "Please Lord protect us from the Devourer." As the name left her lips the man stopped screaming. Confusion began to set in and for the first time in several days Jennifer felt hope return to her heart.

Chapter 13
The Sins of the Past Can Linger

Some things were best left undiscovered.
~ Unknown

Location: Unknown

Gabriel woke with a start to find Othia shaking him. His eyes adjusted to the low light, and even obscured by shadow, he could see the fear on Othia's face. "What's going on?"

He tried to sit up, but the plane shuddered, and he fell back into the seat. He looked toward the cockpit and saw Tim struggling with the controls, so he forced his way up to the front of the aircraft. Othia and Samantha sat helplessly in their chairs. They looked to the water below them that stretched as far as the eye could see.

"What is going on, Tim? It looks like we are having some small issues up here. Care to enlighten us?" Gabriel tried to keep things upbeat, but he couldn't hide the panic in his voice.

Tim spared a brief look at Gabriel, and in that instant Gabriel knew all the information he needed to know. He had seen that look on too many pilots' faces during his time in Afghanistan, and he rushed back to join Othia and Samantha.

"Strap in, now! Don't ask questions, just strap in and pray. We are going too fast, and something is wrong. I didn't ask, but

Tim has enough to deal with. Pray that we hit land, and get *Him* to hear you!"

Gabriel didn't look around. He knew where they were by the disheveled map that he saw thrown in the corner of the cockpit. They had almost made it. They were over halfway there, and now they might die, and so close to their first goal.

A terrified scream from Samantha erupted in the cabin. It was so loud and violent that it drowned out the engines. Her skin paled, and Othia unbuckled her seatbelt to try and comfort her. She looked like she was in shock, and her eyes were fixed on Tim.

The skin of Tim's shoulder hung limply near his neck. Samantha was amazed that it didn't cause him any physical pain. The creature that had crawled out of that wound was nearly the size of a large rat, but that was where the similarities of anything she had seen before ended. The creature's body was covered in fresh gore from the wound, and its matted-down brown hair stuck out at odd angles as it climbed up the back of Tim's neck.

How can he not feel that? Her body was rigid with fear, and her voice was locked away inside her mind, so only her eyes could document the carnage before her.

The creature turned and looked at her. The head of the creature was smashed in on one side, and it looked to be missing half of its jaw. It smiled a broken smile at her and paused to sit on Tim's shoulder. It licked at his earlobe and pulled a small chunk of flesh off his neck. The wound gushed blood, but Tim didn't even flinch to acknowledge that the bite had taken place.

Samantha felt Othia at her side, pawing at her to calm down and trying to get her to talk. She knew that she was scaring her. Hell, she was not exactly enjoying herself right now either.

The creature looked over its shoulder again, and this time it bit the front of Tim's face. The pain from such an attack did not go unnoticed, and screams from the cockpit had Gabriel spinning to try and ascertain what was going on.

Gabriel climbed up into the cockpit and pulled Tim back from the yoke of the plane. The front of his body was covered in blood. Gabriel stared in horror as Tim's eyes were popped by some unseen force. The fluids gushed onto the control panel, and fresh screams filled the small cabin. Gabriel grabbed Tim's body as it shook with spasms, the pain overloading his senses and causing a systematic failure of his organs. Gabriel understood the effects of shock and pain on the human body and rapidly considered what he could do to keep the rest of them alive. Tim's body arched hard, almost bending him completely backward, and then he slammed hard into the control panel. The plane fell forward, pinning Gabriel onto the front glass.

The force of the plane's dive would seal their fate if he didn't act fast. He pushed Tim off the yoke and pulled back on the stick. The plane responded sluggishly. Gabriel felt the panic seeping into his body, and he frantically looked for a solution to their immediate problem. His eyes settled on the automatic pilot switch, and he reached for it to try and save what altitude he could. The plane responded with a little assistance from Gabriel. It leveled out, but as it came under control, sparks and smoke began to erupt from the control panel where Tim's bleeding corpse lay against the instruments. Gabriel knew that he could do nothing about the bodily fluids that had saturated the controls, but he had hoped the automatic pilot function would last longer than it did.

The plane lurched forward again, and Gabriel struggled to keep it under control. He spared a moment to glance behind him. Samantha had closed her eyes and was muttering to herself, and Othia tried to comfort her while also looking at Gabriel for some reassurance that everything was going to be okay.

Gabriel shook his head. "You know how to land a plane?" There was an unusual lack of sarcasm in his voice, and Othia shook her head in reply. "I didn't think so. Well, how hard can it really be? Don't answer that! Just make sure the two of you are strapped in; I see something ahead."

The world screamed by the windows of the small plane as Gabriel fought to control its chaotic descent. He strained to keep it level as the wings seemed to want to shear right off. Samantha and Othia strapped themselves in their seats and began to pray. Neither one knew what to say, but their murmuring could be heard by Gabriel, even over the din of warning indicators in the cockpit. Red and yellow lights illuminated the entire control panel, and he had to brace the yoke with his legs and pull with both hands to get the landing gear to respond.

This was going to be bad, and he knew it. The harness that he had strapped on didn't comfort him, except to assuage his fear of going through the windshield if they came to a sudden stop, but there was no restraint to stop him from dying if the plane exploded when it hit the ground, now, was there? He fought to focus, the muscles in his arms burning under the constant struggle. "Why didn't I spend more time in the gym? God, what I wouldn't give for a little more strength." His humor was lost on everyone in the plane, including himself, and then he spotted the slightly sloping hills on the land directly ahead of them. He had seen them moments earlier when he had taken the controls, and he was trying to steer them toward it. Now they were nearly there, and he didn't know what to do next.

He pushed the nose down gently, hoping to allow the plane to glide in. The metal frame voiced its objections to his current plan by protesting loudly as sparks and smoke began to plague the control panel. "Fire! Othia, get the extinguisher and put this out! I'm stuck here!"

Before he could ask again, Othia shot the foam from the passenger compartment's extinguisher onto the control panel. She was repaid for her efforts with more angry sparks and the plane banking to the right unexpectedly. Her body hit the small bathroom door, and the sound was worse than any injury she could have sustained. Gabriel frantically turned to her, but she waved him off. "Concentrate. I'm fine. Just get us out of this death trap." He didn't give her a reply as he muscled the plane back on course with a new determination.

They were less than fifty feet above the ground. It was not the best he could have hoped for, but at least the grasslands they were coming down on were clear of trees.

"Here we go! I don't know how this will end up, but—" The back of the plane hit the ground first, and Gabriel's mouth slammed shut from the impact. A half second later, the nose of the aircraft hit the uneven ground. The frame of the aircraft moaned and cried as it was torn apart by rocks and changes in the terrain. Samantha watched in horror as the left wing sheared off, sending the plane to the right, and with the wing went several feet of the metal that held the right side of the plane together.

None of them screamed. The crashing metal and wind entering the cabin would have stopped them from hearing each other, but each suffered silently as they rammed into the seats and walls around them. Gabriel's face banged into the side of the cockpit, and brilliant flashes of light erupted in his field of vision. He tasted the metallic streams of blood leaking from his nose, but ignored them. There was nothing he could do but wait. The plane begrudgingly came to a stop as it struck an embankment, smashing the nose into the ground and sending the remains of the tail up into the air. It came close to toppling over, but instead slammed back onto the hard earth.

There was silence for several moments, each of them unwilling to acknowledge that the event was over. Samantha broke the silence asking if everyone was okay. Othla unclipped her seat belt with shaking hands, helping her to her feet, and the two began to inspect the area around them for anything useful. Gabriel shifted Tim's contorted body off of him. He checked the pilot's pulse again, but felt only the still flesh of a dead man. He pulled himself painfully from the cockpit and moved carefully toward the gaping hole in the right side of the plane.

The voices of Othia and Samantha quieted as he emerged from the aircraft. His eyes adjusted to the glare coming off the plane's damaged frame, and he stared in disbelief at the trench he had dug with its mangled metal body. "Not to bring up the obvious, but what the hell just happened?" He looked back in the cabin expectantly at Samantha.

She shook her head. "I don't know. One of those things ripped out of his neck and then dove back inside him." She shivered as she considered going to the front to examine Tim's neck wound.

Sensing what she wanted to do Gabriel changed the topic quickly and glanced at the shattered cockpit window. "We must have slid over seventy yards. How in the hell are we all still alive?" Vicaro's consciousness surfaced for an instant, the arrival of angelic mind sent a chill down his back and gave him a slight headache. The reminder of heavens commitment in the way ahead was clear, causing Gabriel to hold up both hands in mock defeat. "Yeah, I know, I will give due homage to the man upstairs when we are out of the open here."

Gabriel looked back into the cabin and caught Othia's attention, "We need to get out of the open. I want you to take Samantha to the tree line over there. I will be with you in a couple of minutes." He watched as both women gathered their bags, stuffed with new items from the plane, and walked slowly toward the tree line.

Gabriel turned back to the plane, intent on investigating the cargo hold that had not been torn open by jagged pieces of debris or rocks during the crash. It didn't take him long to find what he was looking for, and he smiled to himself. "This guy really was a Boy Scout. Sorry you aren't here to use this stuff, but thanks for always being prepared. This is going to help us a lot."

He pulled out a black cargo pack with red lettering on top, "Survival kit. I never thought I would be happy to see those words together. Let's see what you packed away for a rainy day." Gabriel pulled open the bag and stared at the contents. A new GPS and compass were sitting right on top. There were first-aid supplies and an assortment of knives and fishing equipment. He had never been much for preparing like this, but he was now thankful that Tim had. It would certainly pay off if they ended up stuck here for an extended period of time—wherever *here* was.

Gabriel saw that there had been water in the cargo hold as well, but now there were simply empty plastic bottles. He rounded up some of the bottles and the survival kit and glanced in the cargo hold one last time. He saw some batteries and a flashlight farther back in the rear of the compartment. Gabriel nearly got stuck trying to pull out the flashlight; it was lodged in a section of the tail that was bent at an odd angle from the crash. It was not very forgiving when his hand got stuck between the two bent pieces of the frame.

Gabriel walked to the front of the aircraft and whistled to himself. *Well, if there is a plan for us, God, I believe now that you are at least trying to get us to the start line.* He turned and walked after Samantha and Othia, who were nearing the tree line. Thoughts of Tim's mutilated body and the creature Samantha had said was responsible for it solidified in his mind, adding yet another series of hidden dangers that none of them were made privy to before they set off on their journey.

Chapter 14
Who are the Gatekeepers of the Abyss?

Those who seek shall find; it says so in the Bible so it must be true. Just be careful what you are looking for—it may come with teeth.
~ Unknown

Location: Unknown

Gabriel, Othia and Samantha shivered as their bodies came to grips with their surroundings, their minds finally let go of the trauma from the crash. They all worked as fast as their bleeding fingers would allow crafting their collective shelter for the night. Dark clouds were rolling in, and a slight mist was building around them. It had been cold during their journey across the ocean, but this seemed different. Damp, cold, hungry, and scared, each of them longed for the warmth of shelter and the escape of sleep. The supplies from the kit had come in very handy, and Othia and Samantha were gathering firewood to fend off the chill that was rapidly seeping into their bones.

Each of them was thankful they had continued to purchase extra clothing, as their travels had taken them to colder and colder regions. There was no sign of any sort of civilization. The open grassland they had crashed on was doing little to block the biting wind from entering their small shelter. Othia had to admit, the area was beautiful. She had heard of protected areas where animals roamed free and there were very limited amounts of industrial pollution. It looked as though she was going to experience one of them firsthand, and the vibrant images from the magazines she had brought along allowed for a pleasant distraction from the chaos at hand.

The first few nights were tolerable enough. Gabriel and Othia had found some berries that were edible, and Samantha had located a few wild radishes and turnips that they had all greedily swallowed down in a watery concoction she had created on the fly. When the sun rose on the third day, they decided they needed to push farther into the forests to see if they could find a town or road. Gabriel had found their location on the GPS in the bag, but all it showed was that they had landed on a small uncharted island off the northern coast of Canada.

They walked for hours on end, deeper and deeper into the island. Gabriel shook his head at times as he walked behind the two women. He needed to constantly keep track of Othia, who had a nagging way of becoming lost in thought and wandering off. Samantha, on the other hand, seemed to thrive on their trek through the unknown. He often caught her bobbing back and forth, dancing to music that only she could hear. It was truly the only sense of normalcy the trio had, and Gabriel turned away whenever he thought Samantha was going to look back. Small amounts of normalcy were precious, and he wasn't going to take that away from her due to embarrassment.

They took as many breaks as were needed, and the pace was slow, but they were making progress. After they had walked for about three hours, Othia waded through a collection of fern plants so thick she could almost walk on top of them and came face-to-face with a door. She blinked several times before believing it was really there. The vegetation had taken over the rest of the walls and roof, so it gave the appearance that it was just a door sitting in the middle of nowhere. Othia called up Gabriel and Samantha, and the three stared in open-mouthed fascination at the decaying structures of what appeared to be a small farm community.

Gabriel inspected the door and then shrugged his shoulders. "I guess we better find a way around."

Othia smiled and held out her hands while curtseying to suggest that he take the lead. Gabriel chuckled slightly and bowed slightly. Othia and Samantha fell in behind him as he pushed into the thickets around the door. The walk was treacherous, as they each had to jump over underbrush and grip firmly to the decaying facades to keep from falling into holes that had been created by erosion.

"It looks as though someone tried to wipe this town off the face of the earth, or at least try to erase the fact that people had been here." Othia froze at her words. "Oh my, how did I miss the signs? Both of you, come here. I just remembered something."

Samantha and Gabriel walked over to her and sat down on the soft underbrush as she pulled the book out of her backpack. They shared a confused look as Othia rifled through several pages and then stopped. She looked at them and pointed at the page the book was opened to. "Listen to this: 'Where the stain of man vanishes from the land and only animals remain, the doorway will be unguarded. For what do the watchers fear but the deeds of men and the curiosity within their souls.'"

Gabriel whistled for a long breath, and Othia nodded her head in agreement. "Tell me that doesn't fit this place to a T. I don't know how to explain it, but when you made your comments it came to me, clear out of the blue."

Samantha looked a little uneasy. "If this place is what you say it is, what is running free that those watchers aren't guarding anymore?"

Othia shook her head. "I don't know, but I think we should try and find out. Maybe it is a way out of here. Anything we can do to try and get us off this island is worth looking into."

"Just a question, Othia, but I thought you were supposed to be gifted with some sort of full-fledged knowledge. Why do we still need that book? Didn't you get the full treatment?" The question's lighthearted tone carried the full weight of its accusation.

Othia turned to face Gabriel. "Gabriel, have you ever forgotten something? It's as if all the information is in there, just unorganized. So when things fall into place, it feels as though I have always known the information. But something has to trigger the information into focus. Does that make any sense?"

"You know what, for some strange reason it does. Sorry for asking, but I just needed to know. Thanks."

She nodded and walked forward into the town that was slowly being swallowed by vegetation. The paths were easy enough to traverse. The underbrush had grown over the structures and into the buildings themselves, but the sidewalks and streets were generally left alone. The cobblestones showed general signs of wear, but there wasn't any damage from root systems or weeds growing between the stones. Gabriel glanced at their surroundings and pointed ahead, "I guess we follow the path?"

Samantha and Othia looked at Gabriel with open-ended expressions on their faces. He simply nodded and walked on. They walked for several moments in complete silence, each lost in his or her own assessment of what had happened to the small town they now walked through. They saw modest homes and shops, nothing that stood out as grand, but their construction had stood the test of time, and even though they were severely overgrown, their basic structure was still standing.

Gabriel continued on and glanced over his shoulder, "We should head for the center of town, the main hall or a church. Someplace where they all would have gathered. Maybe we can find some answers there."

"Answers to what? We need to get off this island. Who cares what happened to these people?" Gabriel looked back at Samantha and recognized the haste in her voice for what it was—fear.

"We need to know what happened to find a way out of this, and I think we are supposed to check this out. This all seems a little too exact, don't you think?" said Gabriel.

Othia paused for a moment and nodded, "I have been thinking the same thing. Only I was thinking more so about who was making this happen. If it was one of our friends from the site in Afghanistan, then they would have brought us straight here. Why bother with all the cloak-and-dagger bull? But what if we have been led here by something else?"

Gabriel's skin crawled, and he nodded his head. "No, we are supposed to be here. I can feel it. It feels right for some reason. I don't feel like..." he was about to finish with *like when I am asleep and walk into the pit*, but that was not for them to know about yet. He didn't really know how to put it into words.

Othia smiled. "If you insist, but we should keep our eyes peeled anyway, just in case. This place makes my stomach turn." Samantha moaned her agreement, and they all continued on the path toward what they hoped was the center of town.

The wood-and-clay homes began to grow in size and stature as they moved farther on the path, and soon they could make out a circle up ahead. As they rounded a small curve in the path, they came to what was obviously the center of town, and rays of light cascaded down on the very building they sought. Before them, standing almost untouched by the foliage, was a very old church. Gabriel marveled at how the vegetation had not infested its inner rooms and hallways with underbrush, but Othia's carefully trained eyes spotted something even more unusual.

"Something isn't right here. Look at the base of the building. All the plants that seem to come into contact with it die, and the wood this church is made of hasn't aged like the rest of the town. Either someone is fixing this thing or it is defying the laws of nature right before us."

Each of them stood rooted to the ground in front of the large iron doors that barred their passageway into the inner sanctuary. Othia's words didn't fall on deaf ears: they had sparked the light of Samantha's and Gabriel's imaginations and fanned their worst nightmares into the forefront of their minds. Othia placed a hand on Samantha's shoulder, and Gabriel turned at her startled cry.

Samantha looked foolishly at the ground. "Sorry, my imagination got the better of me. This place is way off the charts of creepiness. I vote we leave and just tell everyone we looked in the creepy church in the middle of nowhere."

Gabriel laughed. "That is probably the best advice we have ever gotten. Let's just look quickly. I don't want to wander aimlessly through the woods. There might be someone or something that can tell us where we can get help."

"I'm worried about the some*thing* part of that."

Gabriel laughed slightly and walked up to the doors, his head craning back. The ironwork was impressive. Standing over seven feet, the doors held ornate carvings each an impressive three feet tall, and while he couldn't say with any certainty, he understood what the artwork portrayed. He had a vague feeling of impending death.

"They almost look like they are in a funeral procession. Look at the two women at the back, one in white and one in black."

Gabriel froze at Samantha's observation. The words from Vicaro ran to the front of his mind: "Watch out for the woman in black." He shrugged it off. Vicaro must have meant a real woman. This situation was just playing with his mind, reaching for conclusions to validate it somehow. After all, this place would scare a writer of horror or any one of those Hollywood horror buffs.

His hand closed around one of the large knockers, and he pushed. The door moved easily, as though it didn't weigh anything. Pain coursed through Gabriel's palm, and he released the knocker with a muffled cry. He looked down and saw that blisters had formed on the skin where it had come into contact with the metal. The injury was not severe, so he simply wrapped it with a piece of his shirt. Othia and Samantha gave him questioning glances, but he simply waved them off. "Sorry, splinter. Should have watched more carefully."

The church's interior was beautiful. The sun spilled through countless stained-glass windows. A trail of footprints followed the trio as they walked through over two hundred years' worth of dust. The remains of thirty or so pews sat rotting in loosely defined rows in the main room. Othia noticed that the dust and the rotting pews were the only sign of the passage of time in the sanctuary. The ceiling was over twenty feet high. At its center was a fresco of the battle for Heaven, and Satan being cast out by the archangel Michael. Gabriel stood motionless, his eyes taking in all the different figures frozen on the ceiling.

Othia joined him. "Look at the corner over there. See the countless figures in the shadows? Those are his armies waiting, always waiting."

"Waiting for what?"

"To attack the Gates of Heaven again, and this time it is said that the victor is unknown, even to those closest to God."

Samantha joined them and glanced up. "What did the writing say above the door, Othia?"

Othia smiled. "Don't miss much, do you?"

Gabriel frowned. He had missed it. "What did it say?"

"'This is the house of our Lord.' Which in and of itself seems innocent enough, and I am sure that is why it went unnoticed by the people in this town."

"It doesn't say who their Lord is."

Othia smiled widely at Samantha, "Looks like there might be an aspiring archeologist among us." The two shared a quick smile and then looked to Gabriel. Samantha continued glancing at Othia to ensure she wasn't overstepping her bounds. "The windows and the fresco seem to all share the common event of Satan's banishment from Heaven. Some of them show his fall, and some show him as a glorious figure, which I am assuming is before his little rumble with the man upstairs."

Othia nodded. "It is in order, beginning at the right side of the front door and working around to the left. The ceiling, I think, is the centerpiece, and the pivotal part of this story."

Gabriel turned and looked behind him. He swallowed hard. "The window on the left is black."

Othia nodded. "Nothingness..."

Her single word echoed in the emptiness of the sanctuary, and each of them knew, but wouldn't admit, that this was the first sound they had truly heard in the confines of the walls. Gabriel looked back. The building didn't look this big from outside. The main worship area seemed to be over fifty feet in length and at least thirty feet wide, which by today's standards wasn't too impressive, but for this forgotten town it seemed very grand indeed.

"What do you make of that?" Gabriel gestured to the far back corner of the main room, where a single door sulked in the corner. Above the doorframe, etched in the stone of the building, was an alcove. Resting comfortably inside were the weathered remains of a statue. Othia walked up and studied the statue, not able to get too close because it remained at the top of the doorframe.

"There is no need to squint, Othia. I'll grab it for you." Samantha took a purposeful step toward the door, and Othia's hand sprang out to hold her fast.

"Don't touch it, Samantha. Don't even look at it. Gabriel, we need to leave this place right now. This isn't a place we are supposed to be in. We are in great danger." Gabriel's expression told Othia that without more information they were not going anywhere. "The statue above the door is a summoning stone. They are also used to enslave sprits to do a person's bidding. This one is of a demon, though not of any one specific spirit that once lived."

"How do you know? The figure is so worn."

"I found this kind of statue once before. The image is still burned into my memory. The horns and keyhole in its mouth are what triggers it. At the beginning of my career, I was on a dig where we uncovered the cities of Sodom and Gomorrah. Our peers scoffed at our discovery, and even with the stone tablets and all the supporting archeological evidence, we could not get them to believe that this was proof that these places did exist and that something very terrible had happened there. We fought for several years to get the recognition we thought we deserved while we were still unearthing the two cities.

"One day, in the center of both cities, we found identical temples that didn't seem to belong to any of the pagan gods of the time and were not consistent with early Jewish temples of the Old Testament times. We were obviously pleased with ourselves and rushed to investigate. I was head of the team going into Sodom, and while I was the youngest of the three archeologists on site, the lead digger liked my ability to keep his men alive, so he used his influence with our sponsor to ensure that at least half of his men would be looked after.

"We entered the temples, and the horrors that we saw were beyond anything I can put into words: bodies long since forgotten about were strewn around, strange animal bones were found in sacrificial chambers, and statues to deities were erected everywhere. One of the statues looked like that." She pointed above the doorframe with her slightly shaking finger.

Othia turned at the sound of Samantha's quivering voice, "What happened to the dig site?"

"We all went in at the same time and tried to gather as much data as possible so our lead archeologist could take some of the initial findings back to Britain to get more funding. We gathered many artifacts and many remains, but I guess we got too greedy.

"On the third day, screams erupted from my dig site, and stories tell that they erupted from our sister site as well. The men who poured out from inside the temple were tearing their own flesh from their bodies in massive chunks, declaring that something was invading their souls. I lost nearly all the men working on my site, and only two remained alive at the other site. When the cries of the men quieted down, they were replaced by the screeching of the wind as a sandstorm hit our camps, burying us beneath three feet of sand. I sought refuge within a cargo truck and waited it out, but the other camp was lost.

"When I made it back to the nearest town, I informed the sponsors of what had happened, and we all agreed to never speak about it and to leave as fast as possible. I swear to you, Gabriel, this statue is just like the one in that temple, and I can feel the presence of something here that isn't necessarily on our side."

Gabriel had felt it as well. "Look, this is the only building not being eaten by vegetation. We need to find a map or something. I am sure these people had to arrive here somehow. Maybe there is a port near here. We just need to know what direction to go in. This place isn't like that temple you found. After all, this place wasn't buried, although it is in the process of it. And if this is a place of our enemy, then let's see if there is anything we can use to defeat them."

"I have seen this look in men's eyes before, Gabriel. Ambition is dangerous, and while I know I will not change your mind, I need one favor."

"Name it."

"I make the rules. If I say we go, there is no argument. This is my profession, and I am damn good at it. So if I say we are done, we walk away, no matter what. Agreed?"

Gabriel stood for a moment and then nodded his head, "Deal."

Chapter 15
Reality Isn't What It Used to Be

And I saw something horrible; I saw neither a heaven above nor a firmly founded earth, but a place chaotic and horrible.
~ Enoch 21:2

Location: Unknown

The trio stood facing the door that would lead farther into the structure of the church.

"Well, what is the game plan?" Gabriel smiled at Othia, and she pushed him toward the door.

"You want to go in so badly, so you open it. But slowly. And we need to find some sort of light source."

Gabriel pulled a small flashlight from his pocket. "A gift from our friend at the diner. I thought he was batty giving it to me, but it looks like he was a lot smarter than I gave him credit for."

Gabriel looked back at his two companions to see if they were smiling, but refocused his attitude when he saw their stern faces staring back at him. His hand gripped the door handle. The cloth around his hand offered a buffer so his skin would not burn again if this metal was the same as on the front door. The question as to what had caused the injury flooded to the front of his mind, and he rapidly pushed it back. It didn't matter why it burned; it only mattered that they find what they were put here for and get out of this crazy place. He paused as a chill ran up his spine while he stood in the doorway.

A click resounded through the open areas of the sanctuary as the door to the room opened slowly. Gabriel marveled at how easily the door swung open. It was even lighter than the doors at the main entrance. That made sense, of course, since this one was drastically smaller, but he didn't need to push it at all. It seemed to *want* to open.

Othia pushed forward and entered the room first. She took note of the simplistic furnishings: a bed; a nightstand; a door at the back of the room, most likely a closet; a cross hanging below a clock; and a painting over the bed's headboard. The wrought-iron work on the headboard was a simple design made to offer elegance on a modest budget. Samantha entered next and moved to the side of the bed nearest the door in the back of the room.

"Samantha, be a dear and see if there is anything behind that door near you." Samantha hesitated for a moment and then saw the kindness in Othia's eyes and turned the handle without a word of complaint. It was empty, a simple closet. There were some rouge dust bunnies in the back corner, and its contents, whatever they might have been, had long been removed from its confines.

As she closed the door behind her, she paused and looked at the handle. *How had she missed it before?* A gasp left her mouth, and Gabriel and Othia turned to see what had startled her. Samantha was squatting before the keyhole for the closet door, but as Gabriel and Othia looked closer they too observed that it wasn't the normal décor usually seen in a church.

There, standing sentry, was a nasty-looking creature with six horns and a large ring attached to the bottom of its mouth acting as the new door handle. Othia noticed a keyhole among the thing's teeth and marveled at its complex design. Gabriel pulled the door open again. He saw for himself that the closet was empty and then took his own inventory of the room. He smiled at the two women, who stood fascinated with the door handle, and he walked over to the center of the room.

"Othia, look at the picture above the bed. Am I really seeing this?" Gabriel pointed at the oil painting hanging above the headboard directly in front of Othia.

"I noticed it, but I don't know really what to make of it. It is a depiction of this room, exactly as you would see it if you were standing at the door. The detail is uncanny and..." She paused for a moment. "Look, the clocks match in both of them. They're stopped at one."

"What is that below the painting? Looks like some sort of poem written in block letters?" Samantha got closer, but Othia pulled her back.

"It's French, and it looks like it was written with crayon or chalk of some kind. Has nothing in this place aged?"

Othia looked back at Gabriel, and he answered with a simple shrug. "What does it say?"

Roses are blue

Violets are Red

Knock at the door for you know who

If you choose to knock three times

Those behind can show you the divine

But caution should be taken here

For knocking can wake that which you fear

To all those too foolish to leave

Come on in, I have set the tea

"Well, isn't this an interesting development we have here?" Gabriel shrugged his shoulders again and then walked over to the door in the corner of the room and pulled it open. "Just a closet here. And truthfully, there isn't anything inside, just some old tattered dirt devils and empty shelves."

Samantha shifted uneasily at the entrance of the room, and Othia gently took her hand. "What is the matter? You are getting a little pale."

Samantha turned and looked at Othia. Her warm smile did little to placate the uneasy feelings that were running through the pit of her stomach. She shook her head. "I have a weird feeling that I can't shake. I guess it is all the stress finally catching up with me. But doesn't this place feel out of whack? I mean, like it is off base or something. I can't describe it, but I really feel it."

Othia thought for a moment. "There is something here that feels a bit different, but every time I try and pin it down, a sense of calm washes over me. Maybe it is like you said, just stress."

Gabriel walked over to join them. "Well, the room is empty, and this is the only door I saw in the sanctuary. Any ideas?"

Samantha nodded, "Yeah, I have one, but I don't think we should play it out. Something feels wrong."

Gabriel looked at her, "Well, let's hear it and then we can all decide."

Samantha looked at the floor, "Knock."

Gabriel felt like he should laugh, but the idea had crossed his mind also. When he looked at Othia, he knew that the riddle was making its way into her thoughts as well. "Before we do that, any ideas as to what we are going to find?"

Othia and Samantha both shrugged their shoulders and then Othia said, "The words are an old French dialect, so I would say that this place is about three to four hundred years old. But I have never seen anything survive like this at any dig site, ever. One thing I do know is this is the end of the line if we stop here."

Gabriel thought for a moment and then stepped behind the two women. He shut the door and looked over his shoulder.

"Well, let's start knocking, unless there are any objections." Samantha caught the words before they could leave her mouth. She knew they shouldn't, but she couldn't put the right words together. *Has to be nerves*, she told herself, and she watched as Gabriel raised his hand to knock on the door they had just walked through.

The three knocks on the door echoed in the small room, which made each of them share uneasy glances. Gabriel reached for the door handle, and Othia stayed his hand. She pulled out the gun from her jacket and then nodded back to Gabriel. He shifted his weight back so he could get out of the way should Othia feel the need to shoot when he opened the door, and took in a long breath. "One, two, three!" With all his might, Gabriel pulled open the door and quickly stepped out of the way.

He watched Othia raise the pistol and then relax her shoulders, "Nothing. What is so nerve-racking about this?"

"Well, considering all that has happened lately, I guess we really can't say for sure what we will find."

Othia looked over at Samantha and nodded approvingly. "I think we have a thinker on our hands, Gabriel."

"Good, at least one of us is using their head. Let's try the closet door." The trio moved to take up their identical positions at the closet door, and again Othia relaxed as the blank wall stared back at her.

Gabriel shut the door and began to walk back toward the door that would lead out to the sanctuary. "Well, that was interesting. Maybe there are some clues in one of the other buildings in town." He pulled open the door, but stopped when Samantha's words gave him pause.

"Wait, we are missing something." Samantha stood at the foot of the bed and was staring at the painting and the inscription. "Look at the inscription. It is under the painting, not near one of the doors. It makes reference to a door, but why put it there if you needed to knock on the ones in the room?" Gabriel and Othia both looked at one another and simply nodded in agreement with Samantha's logic. "Gabriel, this is going to sound odd, but knock on the *painting's* door." She saw the questioning look on Gabriel's face and she could only encourage him to try. "Please, what can it hurt, since we are out of options with the two doors in the room?"

Gabriel moved toward the painting and placed one foot on the bed so he could reach the door painted on the fabric. His hand froze for a moment and then it came down on the painted door. The dull thud of his striking the wood behind the fabric slightly startled him, and he felt childish. The two women watched, and then a flicker of light caught their eyes. The cross under the clock on the wall had burst into flames. The flames burned bright and changed from blue to orange, and then red in a matter of moments, turning the cross to burnt embers. Gabriel drew his sword from his back, and Othia raised her revolver and waited for anything out of the ordinary to happen. An uneasy silence filled the room as they waited.

"We need to knock again. It said three times." Samantha was startled at the sound of her own voice breaking the silence.

Gabriel looked at his companions and saw they were both in agreement, and he faced back toward the painting. He raised his hand again and let it fall on the canvas. The thud was louder this time as his hand struck the board behind the painting. A slight tremor shook the room, and Othia felt fingernails dig into her forearm. She glanced at Samantha and saw panic etched on her face.

"What is it? What is—" The words stopped in her throat as she looked down at the bed. The white sheet was turning red with blood. As the form of a man began to take shape, she shook her head in disbelief. "This can't be."

Gabriel looked down and gasped. "Othia, what am I looking at here? And why are we not running out of this room right now?" The room was quiet with only their collective breathing breaking the oppressive silence.

"I don't believe it. This looks like the shroud that covered Christ when he was placed in his burial cave. But this can't be..." Othia's voice trailed off, and Samantha gave Gabriel a worried look.

"That's it, Samantha. Open the door. I'll get Othia. We are out of here."

Samantha moved toward the door that had closed while the three had been looking at the painting on the wall. Othia, still transfixed by the image that was becoming more and more evident on the bedsheet, seemed to be listening to something that the others could not hear. Gabriel placed his hand on her forearm, intent on pulling her away, when he heard Samantha heave a worried sigh. He turned and saw her pulling at the door handle. "What's up? Stuck or something?" Her worried look told him things were not going their way, but when he looked into the doorway he was not ready to see the bricks that stared back at him. "Okay, I'm not the smartest guy, but I know that we didn't walk through that coming in here. Othia?"

Othia tore her gaze from the bed and looked slack-jawed at the doorframe. Samantha looked over her shoulder and saw a shape rising up from the bed and filling out the image that they had seen etched in blood.

"Are you fucking kidding me right now? Gabriel!"

Samantha's hushed warning was enough to spin Gabriel toward the bed, and he immediately saw what had spooked her. He hurriedly looked for any other exit, but before he finished scanning the room his gut told him the picture was their only hope of getting out of the room before who or whatever was in the bed tore off the sheet. He pushed Othia and Samantha to the corner of the room opposite the closet door and turned back to face the painting.

"Shit, shit, shit." He didn't need Samantha's whispered warning to tell him the thing in the bed was still rising and taking on more of a human shape with each passing breath. *One more knock, and this either goes crazy or we get out of this in one piece.* Gabriel's hand tapped against the fabric. He heard a dull knock on the wood behind the painting, and in a fleeting instant, he couldn't breathe as the form on the bed began to shake violently.

He almost thought he had imagined it. The ghastly form coming out of the bed stood nearly six feet tall when it began to thrash back and forth. With a sickening pop, a geyser of blood and gore shot toward the ceiling. As the viscous fluid continued to erupt none of the vile substance came back down. Instead it pooled like a swirling oil painting overhead. He couldn't look away. Disbelief turned to fear as he saw the terror on both of his companions' faces. Their fear spread through his veins rapidly, and he looked around the room again. At the back of his thoughts his mind was telling him something was coming. The body on the bed was clearly a distraction; but for what? *What it was coming?*

Gabriel looked at Othia. "Anything in that book of yours about something like this?" He saw the hint of recollection in her eyes, and she went hurriedly to her bag. He watched as she frantically tried to open her satchel that carried her gift. When her attempts failed, Samantha lent her frustrated hands to the equation. He felt a cool breeze enter the room his eyes going instantly to the pool of gore above them—the ceiling was different. It had grown to over twenty feet. When they had entered, it had been only ten or so

The stench of blood and rotting flesh rose on the cool breeze, and the three turned to face the closet door, each with a look of disbelief on his or her face. Gabriel felt a warm tingle in his mind and on his back, and before his mind could grasp the movement, his sword was off his back and radiating a soft white light in his hand. He turned to face the opposite corner of the room, and it seemed to shimmer. Gabriel did a double take and caught the strange play of lights again.

"What the hell is that in the corner?"

A deafening roar was his answer; Gabriel stood motionless as he watched a black jagged hole appear in midair, almost as though the room wasn't real, just a piece of paper that you could tear out of a magazine. His mind reeled in the process of trying to comprehend what he was looking at, and a knot of fear turned in his stomach. Staring directly into the most complete blackness he had ever seen, his eyes focused on a figure that was pulling itself out of nothingness and beginning to take shape before him. It was a creature that he had only heard of in nightmarish stories as a child, stories of demons and vile creatures that manned the pits of Hell, waiting for children who misbehaved or were found unacceptable by God.

As vivid as the memories were, they could not have captured the raw corruption and hate that emanated from the thing now standing before him. It swayed from side to side on two massive legs. Clawed feet dug into the floor as its monstrous weight shifted, and they let out a jaw-wrenching scratching noise that seemed to grate against Gabriel's bones. His eyes took in the immense body that stood over fifteen feet tall and took up almost the entire wall when its huge rotted wings unfurled behind its back. A chaotic landscape of cuts and diseased wounds covered the creature's torso. Its enlarged limbs bulged with muscle and scar tissue, showing the creature's immense strength, both physical and mental, to endure the endless pain that must have accompanied the innumerable wounds on its body. Rotting skin tore in several places on the creature's wings, and sores opened on the thing's arms and legs, oozing yellow and green pus onto its dark red skin. Its head was what terrified Gabriel the most: it looked like the shape of a human skull but much larger. He could see fangs jutting out from inside its mouth, and a shaggy mane of blood-matted hair covered one of the piercing eyes that looked directly into his soul. He heard cries of alarm, and he knew that Othia and Samantha could see it as well.

"Move toward the closet. Now!" The trio made their way cautiously toward the closet door. Othia reached for the handle, and another roar echoed in the small room. Gabriel turned rapidly toward the creature with his sword held at the ready.

The creature shook back and forth with a guttural laugh. "*Shal wanakini, foos lalll.*"

Gabriel turned to Othia, who was struggling with the door to the closet. "What is it saying?"

She paused for a moment and let Samantha pull on the handle. She looked directly at Gabriel, ignoring the creature looming only a few feet away. "It said, 'That piece of shit pig sticker won't help you fight me.'" Her eyes didn't waver, and Gabriel felt the twisting knot of fear in his stomach grow.

"Get it open and get inside. I can keep it busy for a minute or two to let you both get in, if it comes to that." Gabriel's confidence sounded reassuring, but Othia heard the hidden note of fear in his voice. She turned without another word, and Gabriel was left alone to face the creature. Its body was now only a few feet away.

Gabriel's eyes came to rest on the weapon in the creature's clawed hands. He had never seen a blade that large before. The rusted piece of steel looked to be a tremendous cleaver measuring over eight feet. Faint light from the only lamp in the room caught the large gashes in the steel that were evidence of the countless centuries of warfare the weapon had seen.

Without warning, the creature lunged at Gabriel. He thrust the sword up to meet the incoming cleaver. The speed of the blade compensated for Gabriel's momentary stunned reaction, but the strength behind the attack sent him slamming into the wall. Othia and Samantha cried out in terror, and Othia swore aloud. Amid the screaming pain inside Gabriel's head, he distinctly heard the metallic click of a door unlocking. His blurred vision cleared, and he looked between Samantha and Othia into the doorway that had once led into the closet.

The doorway was now an entrance to some sort of tunnel system. A staircase wound down into the darkness. It was flanked by two mammoth statues of angels that wore the same armor as those Othia and he had seen in Afghanistan. The stone sentries were enough to make him pause and stare at their majesty, only pulling his mind and vision away when his sword arm again met the crushing blow of the demon creature. Gabriel heard tendons pop in his arm, and fresh flashes of pain shot up and down his body.

Othia and Samantha grabbed his shoulders and pulled him into the doorway. A thunderous metallic strike echoed in the room. The demon had just missed him, and it roared angrily as it fought to free its weapon from where it was now embedded in the floor. Gabriel swallowed hard. His legs had been where the blade had struck only a fraction of a second earlier.

Othia dropped Gabriel's shoulder, and he fell unceremoniously to the ground. Samantha nearly followed him but caught herself at the last moment. Othia rushed to the doorframe and began to read the strange writing. There was a shudder in the entryway and then the sound of chain falling. The creature tore its blade free, taking several large chunks of the floor with it, and took one massive stride toward the closet door. It had bent down and begun to push its head into the doorway when a gate slammed into the ground in front of it, shattering the stone with its impact. A deafening roar spilled from the mouth of the creature. It bit, clawed, kicked, and slammed its murderous weapon into the gate in a frenzied effort to destroy the one obstacle in its way.

Gabriel watched as each blow from the demon's claws hit the gate and caused the strange writing on the doorway to flare bright white. Chunks of wall and floor sailed over the demon's head and landed behind it as the beast demolished the room they had just departed from. Othia turned and faced her friends, the strains of a panicked heart etched in her eyes.

"Where is he? The boy that was by the door, where is he? Did you see him come in here?" Confused, Gabriel and Samantha looked at one another.

Gabriel got up, rushing over to Othia, and placed his hands on her shoulders. He looked at the creature still bellowing on the other side of the gate and pulled her a few more feet away from the door. "Othia we have to move, what boy? The only ones here are the three of us and that thing. You figured out the door and let us in. That damn thing nearly took my legs off. Come on we have to move. Thank goodness you were such a quick study."

Othia shook her head in frustration letting Gabriel take her hand and pull her deeper into the passageway. "I didn't figure it out. There was a little boy that just appeared. He pointed at the release and the door opened. I would have never found it in time. I saw him run in here, but lost him after I closed the gate. Oh my God, he must have gone down the stairs. We have to go after him!"

Gabriel gripped her hand tightly, "No one went down the stairs. But hey, don't take our word for it, let's get a look for ourselves." He noticed that even with all the debris that the creature had knocked loose there were no other footprints except their own. Not allowing anything to distract them Gabriel continued to pull Othia down the stairs.

A roar from the doorway as they were nearly out of sight pulled Gabriel's attention back to the ornate gate. The creature was still tearing apart the room on the other side, but his murderous eyes were locked on the trio. He could see the color changing in the center of the creature's eyes, as though molten lava was swirling around in them.

"*Yone canno waktl affhe. A finale ppaene.*"

Gabriel looked at Othia, and she simply stared at the irate demon. Her voice was crystal clear over its cries as she translated the demon's words for the benefit of her friends. "'You cannot keep me from my prize, flesh puppets. I will enjoy feasting on your souls as your bodies are stripped of their flesh in the seas of razor blades.'" Samantha felt an icy-cold chill run down the length of her spine, but Gabriel simply nodded and looked around the chamber at their new surroundings.

"Is there any way we can shut the door on this thing, so that we don't have to hear it threatening us? I am pretty sure we understand what it wants to do."

Othia, her eyes still glazed over, pointed at a section of wall that looked different from the rest. "Pull on the right side, and it will slide over the gate and seal us in." Gabriel paused and looked at her. She seemed heartbroken, as though she was remembering something that cut deep into her soul.

Samantha made a motion as though she was intending to rush back up the stairs. "We are not closing this. We won't be able to get out."

"I don't want to beat around the bush on my own inadequacies here, so I won't: I can't beat that thing out there, and if we leave here it is going to kill us. Now, I for one don't really want to have that happen. There has to be another way out of here. That thing wouldn't be so pissy if we were just going to rot in here."

Samantha eyed him cautiously, not truly believing him fully. The creature's guttural roar cut off her thinking, she sprinted to the top of the stairs and pulled on the corner of the wall herself. The texture was light and strong under her fingers, and as she pulled, the wall slid into place over the gate. A large clank brought about more roars of frustration from the demon, but they were muffled now and seemingly growing more distant.

Chapter 16
Watch Out for the Things That Go Bump in the Night

Man's heart can be corrupted if a weakness can be found.
~ Gospel of the Fallen 45:19

Location: Unknown

The chamber had acted as an entryway to something. Gabriel had no idea what, but he had gathered that much. His brief glimpse of the statues that flanked the stairway were impressive their memory seemed to pull at his mind.

They now sat at the bottom of first staircase. The demon now a distant echo up the stairs seemingly far away, but never far enough. The stairs emptied onto a small landing and continued into darkness further into the subterranean depths. It was only a brief stop to try and gain their bearings, so they weren't fumbling into yet another danger around the corner. Samantha gently took Othia's hand and lifted up her chin. She looked at her kindly. "What is the matter? We're okay. And I think Gabriel is right: we will find a way out of here. We just have to...have faith."

The end of her statement sounded forced, but Othia didn't seem to notice. She simply nodded and smiled wearily. "I remember..." Her words were barely audible, and both Gabriel and Samantha looked at her.

"Remember what, Othia?" Gabriel walked over and joined the two women, who were now sitting on the floor.

Othia shook her head. "The little boy, I know where I saw him before. He was at the dig site. He gave me a torch to enter the first chamber. I remember his eyes; they were so blue. I admit it didn't strike me at the time, but when I saw him this time, it was as though there was no need to question what was going on, just to do as he showed me."

Samantha looked worriedly at Gabriel. He nodded and tried to assess their options. He wanted to keep going, to try and put space between them and that thing in the other room. The demonic roars were fading and is gut told him they were pretty safe, for now. There was only one way into this area now, and they could stand watch. Something in the ceiling was making light, so he assumed they should be able to see for as long as they needed to stay here. "Let's all just take a little breather. We can rest in shifts, and we will keep looking around after we all have had a little break."

Samantha eased Othia down and cradled her head so she could relax more freely.

"I'll take the first watch. You two rest as well as you can," said Gabriel. He looked at Othia for a moment and saw her hand go to her neck again. She was unconsciously scratching at that same spot. He gently took her hand and pulled it away. "Remember, we can't get to a corner store, so let's try not to infect it. Mind if I take a look?"

She simply stared back at him, and he took her silence as consent. He pulled down her collar slightly and saw a dark red rash localized under the bone-carved pendant she wore around her neck. The design was strikingly odd. It looked like the letter C with an incomplete triangle in it. With fingers outstretched, he moved to remove the source of Othia's irritation, but her icy fingers gently closed around his hand before it came in contact with the pendant.

"No, this is for me to bear…"

Gabriel thought the construct of what she said was strange, but he dismissed it and stood again. He knew they would have to keep tabs on the rash so that it didn't spread, but if she wanted to wear the pendant, so be it.

He paced up and down the stairs, constantly checking on the sealed entry way. The walls seemed to be carved out of solid stone. In fact, he couldn't find a single seam to show where the gate had been. A smile crossed his face as he glanced again at the statues standing sentry over the stairs. One bore a striking resemblance to Abaddon; the smug look was a dead giveaway. The other warrior looked fearsome—not to say that his gut didn't twist when he looked at Abaddon, but this unknown counterpart looked as though his wrath was beyond reason.

Hours passed. Gabriel woke Samantha to take watch when his eyes seemed to consistently defy his demands to stay open. He gave her a very brief refresher class on how to work the pistol. She only needed to fire one shot, and all of them would be awake in an instant. Gabriel didn't bother to discuss the possibility that any shooting in here might cause a bullet to ricochet and hit one of them. It was there to make Samantha feel safe, not to really accomplish anything. The stone floor seemed a gift from the heavens as he stretched out on it. His bones and muscles felt ancient, each one reminding him how his procrastination about getting back into shape was a very bad idea. Sleep came quickly to his mind and body. There was no endless wasteland to greet him, no blood-drenched skyline that rushed into view or creatures sulking in the shadows, only the darkness of exhaustion.

Even with the light emanating from its unknown source in the ceiling, the shadows seemed to grow while Samantha walked slowly around the room. Her footfalls were silent, only disturbing the dust covering the floor that had not seen anyone in quite some time. The gun felt heavy, and she was constantly trading hands, always cautious not to point it at anyone and to keep her finger off the trigger. Man, she hated these things. *It's okay. Everything will be okay. There is nothing to worry about.* Patronizing herself was one of her best attributes, but even that seemed to fail her now. Her eyes rested on the statues for the hundredth time. There truly was little else to look at. The steps were out of the question: her mind would race as soon as her eyes took a glance at the first step. It always brought forth images of strange, creepy-crawly things that were intent on eating all of them. No, she would look at the statues, and that was all.

A dull red light began to fill the room, and she froze midstride. The lights had never done that before, and the feeling that was slowly filling her insides was nothing short of dread. She settled her eyes on the face of the angel that Gabriel had called Abaddon. His stern features and broad armor made her feel safe for some reason. The features of his face and the unmistakably brutal nature of the sword he carried suggested that perhaps she should run and hide, but she felt as though the statue was there to protect them. The other one was another story altogether. The red light seemed to be coming from behind the statue of the unnamed warrior. Its wings were bathed in the blood-colored illumination. Her eyes wouldn't settle on the statue's eyes. The ornate armor it wore around its neck was as close as she could get to looking at the stone giant's face. It was impossibly elaborate. She fought to find a flaw in any of the beautifully carved armor, but her sight was immediately lost in its intricate detail.

Her mind came back to the present when the hair on the back of her neck began to rise. Something was wrong, and she spun around the room to find out what was causing her body to panic so. As she whirled, she felt a burst of hot air erupt from the depths of the staircase. Her hair whipped into her eyes, and she was temporarily blinded. She fought with frantic fingers to clear her vision.

As her hands cleared away the strands of hair that battled to cover her face, her heart stopped. Samantha's gaze froze on

Gabriel, resting on the ground. His body was completely still and lying flat on his back. Her eyes filled with tears of utter fear as she looked at the creature hovering above him with outstretched claws. The creature was covered with rotting flesh, and as its fingers settled onto Gabriel's forehead and neck, its teeth parted in an unsettling hiss. Milky white eyes rolled in its head. They had no irises; only bloodshot veins provided any contrast to the stark white orbs. Her hand tightened around the pistol's hand guard as she brought it up. The barrel lay flush with the creature's back.

She was only ten feet away, but her confidence in hitting the creature was diminished by the mounting terror that raced in her blood. The thing's odor saturated the small area, and she felt her knees weaken as small eruptions of bile shot up her throat. Gabriel's instructions swept into her mind, "You only have to fire one shot, and we will wake right up." The words came like a shockwave to the front of her consciousness, breaking her paralysis, and the gun went off. The creature snarled and turned to face her. Its twisted face was a mask of hate and pain. She saw gray sludge leaking onto the floor from the creature's back where she had hit it, but Gabriel still did not stir.

Othia woke and sat bolt upright, reaching inside her bag for the gun that lay in Samantha's hand. Her eyes took a moment to adjust and then the air was sucked from her lungs in utter shock.

Samantha saw the movement and heard her gasp. Her tear-streaked face turned toward Othia, and she simply shook her head. "Cast it out, Othia. Hurry! It is doing something to him. Cast the damnation back to—" her words were lost in a scream that erupted from her lips as she sailed through the air and slammed into the opposite wall.

The creature finished with Gabriel and pulled itself on the floor toward the nowunconscious form of Samantha. Her body lay in a broken heap on the other side of the entryway. Othia's eyes looked frantically from Samantha to Gabriel. Her vision settled on Gabriel's backpack, where the shotgun resided, and she tried to force her body to respond, to jump up and lunge for it. She simply sat rigid with fear as the creature twisted to focus its attention solely on her.

Othia's hands fought off the effects of shock and weariness as her mind commanded them to manipulate the pages of her book as fast as they could. The incantations and prayers flew through her mind as she fought against time itself to find the right weapon to fight this thing that was now attacking them. She heard a series of pops and tears and looked up from her frantic search. The creature was stuck on something that protruded from the floor and was literally pulling its legs off to continue its quest for the unconscious Samantha.

Othia's hands still flipped the pages, even without the assistance of her eyes. Her search stopped abruptly, and her hands rested on a spread of ornate pages within the sacred text. Her voice radiated across the room and reached the depths of the chambers they still had yet to explore below. "In the name of Christ and God the Father, leave this place at once. You wretched filth, you will depart our presence. For we are the Thirteenth Legion, and we will send you back to Hell where the torments inflicted on the wicked are for the glory of God!"

The creature came to a stop and turned to face her. Its gray, rotting flesh and visible innards were covered with countless wounds, but still it turned and began to crawl toward her. She repeated the words again, and the creature recoiled in pain. Its legs, now a few feet behind it, shook as well. The thing bared its unholy maw at Othia. Its rotting teeth had been replaced with jagged pieces of bone pushed into its decomposing gums.

Othia shouted the words again, but gagged as a wave of fluid and tissue spewed forth from the deformed creature, clogging her mouth and eyes. She felt her own vomit mix with the creature's projectile bile as it poured down the front of her body. Her eyes burned, and she thought she could hear a hiss as the exposed skin on her face and arms burned. She felt a skeletal hand grip her thigh, and she fought frantically to break its grasp. Her shirt ripped. She felt another mushy hand touch her stomach, and she screamed.

A voice boomed in the small chamber, and the creature stopped. "In the name of Christ and God the Father, leave this place at once. You wretched filth, you will depart our presence. For we are the Thirteenth Legion, and we will send you back to Hell where the torments inflicted on the wicked are for the glory of God!"

Othia felt the creature's hands leave her body, and she heard a series of sickening snaps and pops. She fought frantically to clear her eyes to see what was going on. As her vision improved, she saw the blurred form of Samantha slumped over the stone foundation of one of the angelic statues. White light appeared to be coming from the back of its wings, and Othia could almost swear she saw small amounts of smoke wafting off of Samantha's clothes. She looked unconscious again, but her broken body had moved—that much was for certain. But that had not been her voice. It couldn't have been. The tone, clarity, and power were like nothing she had ever heard before.

She pushed herself up and looked at the puddle of decomposing flesh and bones that rested a few feet from her. The hiss and pop of rotting flesh immersed itself in her ears, and she fought to rid herself of the smell, taste, and sounds of this foul creature that had attacked them. Her body refused to move fast, but she pushed as hard as it would allow to get to Samantha's side.

Samantha's body was cold to the touch, and she gently pulled her off the stone slab and laid her body onto the floor. She was a wreck. How she had even moved was unknown to Othia. Both legs were swollen, seemingly broken, and her right arm was bent at an unnatural angle. Othia had been around enough death in her life to know that these wounds would mean the end of her friend if she didn't do something.

She hurriedly looked around the room and saw Gabriel still lying on his back. His chest rose and fell faintly. "What did they do to you?" Her question was lost in the chaos of the recent events.

She held Samantha's head in her lap until she seemed to be resting as comfortably as possible in her unconsciousness and then moved to study her text. Some enlightened person she was. Where was this divine knowledge that was supposed to help them? Curses flew from her lips as she tore through pages, desperately looking for answers for how to bring Gabriel back and how to cure the wounds of Samantha.

Chapter 17
Nothing in Life is Given for Free. What Price are you Willing to Pay for That Which You Think you Need?

Though the devil is the Great Deceiver, man has studied his tactics throughout history. And just as there are those who wish to emulate Christ there are those who wish to emulate the Morning Star.
~ Unknown

Location: Port Angeles, Washington, USA

Secure, powerful, and tenacious high-heel strikes filled the hallways leading to the detective offices at the Port Angeles Police Department. Modest remodeling kept the 1960s building functional, but city officials never cared enough to invest in making it attractive.

Cincaid walked briskly down the hallway. Her tailored pantsuit hugged her body perfectly, and she privately enjoyed the shocked stares her peripheral vision caught. She had been told that expensive clothes always fit better. She could hardly argue with the disarming results her wardrobe presented. Recent encounters with her lord Uther were fueling her passions and though murder held a special place in her heart she understood the value in the sensual manipulation of men.

Not her most favored infiltration technique; however there was a certain flattery with this approach she didn't mind. The desk sergeant nearly fell out of his chair when she walked in and flashed her Federal Bureau of Investigation identification. The immaculately designed forgery passed the cursory inspection of the officer. As he attempted to give her directions to the upstairs offices, his eyes continued to take in her exposed skin and curves.

Cincaid held a black leather briefcase that contained documents detailing all the activities she had personally overseen the last three years. Uther had ordered her to drop off the documentation as official FBI files and to offer what limited insight she saw fit to the specifically named detective. Uther wanted to energize the local police to find Gabriel and the missing archeologist; however, she failed to see the logic with this course of action. Uther's frustration with the federal government and their own private efforts were forcing his hand to try less frequently used channels.

He had tried to assuage her fears, telling her that even if the police could draw all the conclusions, the Assembled would be completely shielded. Nothing in the reports suggested anything other than maddening data of horrific crimes she had planned and seen through. Uther had also told her that even if these documents were used to substantiate an unknown case against the Assembled, this was the perfect opportunity to defraud that investigation. The interdiction of falsified reports would taint any investigation, and once again the Assembled would be protected by the congested legal system of the United States. As the rationalization of Uther's plan ran through her mind, she relaxed. She knew that he would never place her or the Assembled in jeopardy. It was unwise to question Uther's actions. Somehow any emergence of the slightest faltering in faith from his followers was always discovered and punished severely.

Her eyes focused on the door ahead and the thoughts of her disagreement with Uther's plan faded from the front of her mind. She pushed open the door and glanced around the room. Uther had been very specific: she was to approach a detective with the first name of Matthew. No one else was capable of accomplishing his agenda. She quickly evaluated the four men who stood in the room, each lost in a mountain of paperwork. The description Uther had given her was exact. The man was mid-twenties, Caucasian, just over six feet tall, and of modest build. She spotted him instantly. He wore a gray suit, one that could be used for all occasions, and that gave him a somewhat polished look, but Cincaid paid it little attention. As she entered the room, the clamor from her high heels caught the attention of the three other men in the room, and each of them stared in silent envy as she walked up to their colleague's desk. Green eyes stared up at her, and she smiled inwardly, keeping her face an unreadable mask of professionalism.

"May I help you, ma'am?"

"Your name is Matthew, correct?" Cincaid waited for a moment as the man simply nodded his head. "Then yes, you can help me. Your boss must have some pretty powerful people in his corner. I am Special Agent Carmik, and I was ordered to personally deliver the contents of this parcel to you." Cincaid slammed the briefcase onto the desk and opened it rapidly. She pulled out the large stack of files and dropped them squarely on the man's desk. "This is everything my office has been tracking for the last three years. Your attorney general and governor want you to make this a priority, which is fine by me."

The detective looked confused for a moment, and Cincaid began to grow frustrated. This guy was supposed to be sharp—as if any of them were. "Listen, I don't have a lot of time here. You requested information that cross-references a certain symbol and modus operandi of a case you are working on. Well, this is your lucky day. Here it is. Don't bother saying thank you. I can show myself the way out."

She turned to leave, and finally the man jumped up, "Ma'am, I am sorry. This is just such a huge break. What was your name again?"

"Special Agent Carmik."

"Well, Special Agent Carmik, thank you for this. My boss is looking for some sort of pattern or correlation, and this is going to blow his mind. It's going to take me a while to comb through this, but we truthfully can use all the support we can get. Is there anything in here I should pay specific attention to? There is a lot of data here."

Cincaid was pleased the man had finally come out of his shell, but she pressed the disgruntled federal employee persona further, "Look, I am a ten-year veteran of the Bureau, and I have just been reduced to a courier. So forgive me if I don't feel like staying and chatting. I have seven cases I am working, and all of them have been placed on the back burner so I can personally deliver this to you. Now, do you have any educated questions to ask?"

Matthew was taken aback and simply shook his head.

"Fine, you will find all the data correlated chronologically. The trail is simple to follow, but the motive is very convoluted, if tangible at all. I am sure you will find what you are looking for since you have the ability to divert more analytical power to it than we have. The only direction I can give you is to find whomever it is you are looking for quickly, Detective. All the information I have been looking at suggests that the persons you seek are a very dangerous group indeed."

With that, she turned and walked out of the office with an air of contempt for the police station. The rhythm of her stride reverberated through the station until she exited through the front door, where the desk sergeant's lingering eyes nearly caused him to wear the cup of coffee he was drinking.

Chapter 18
Knowledge is the Most Intoxicating Freedom and the Most Vile Prison

And the world shall bow before us upon our day of victory, for we shall not only be in their minds but possess their souls as well.
~ Gospel of the Fallen 98:12

Location: Unknown

    Mist from Othia's frantic breaths nearly blocked her sight of the pages before her. The temperature in the entry chamber seemed to be falling sharply with each passing minute. The crisp sound of book pages turning filled the chamber as Othia's fingers flew through each of them, trying desperately to find any passage that might aid her two wounded friends. Desperation had plagued her mind for the better part of three hours as she discovered the blank spots in her newfound knowledge ever expanding in the most needed areas. She told herself that it was simply fatigue setting in and that the information would jump off the pages when she came upon it. But this was her second time through the mammoth book, and no answers had surfaced yet.

    A soft breeze caressed the back of her neck, and she turned to look longingly down the stairwell behind her. Delusions of grandeur filled her mind as her gaze stared into the depths of the unknown. She envisioned frantically searching the lower chambers to find a cure for Gabriel and medicine for Samantha. The thoughts paraded through her mind and distracted her from the important mission at hand.

Her hand slammed down on the book, and her eyes snapped back to the front. She stared down at intricate artwork that depicted a horrid-looking beast standing over a man's body. The tips of her fingers touched the title of the passage, and her hands began to shake slightly. "Possession of the Thirteenth." Her voice was scarcely above a whisper, but it reverberated through the small chamber and spilled down the stairwell. She waited in anxious silence, listening to her voice fade into the depths of the farthest reaches of the chamber directly below her.

Her eyes skimmed the page, and the parallels of her current situation and the example given in the text as background information were eerily similar. Othia devoured the information: the book's demonic markings, the list of symptoms, and the description of the moment of infliction. She stopped mid-paragraph and rushed over to Gabriel's side and tore open his shirt. Her breath rushed out of her lungs when she saw the markings that were illustrated in the book burned onto his skin. She scooped up the ancient text and read further into the pages.

"The word of God is the most powerful force in all creation. His children, since the dawn of time, have tried to imitate His power through their own manipulation of His voice. Their successes have been limited in capability compared to the original; however, they still have had devastating results in their mutated state. The closer the language is to that of the Creator, the more powerful it will become. Only those words from the Almighty Himself can counteract those of children whom He created first."

Othia swallowed hard and looked at Gabriel's complexion. He was starting to fade fast. Her ears caught the sounds of Samantha's labored breathing, and knew she needed to get them some sort of help, regardless of the cost. The book had answered the cause of Gabriel's condition, but not given her the remedy. Her hands tore open Gabriel's bag. She gripped the sawed-off shotgun and pocketed some extra shells from the antique box. She looked back at her friends lying helpless and then took two determined steps toward the stairwell.

As her foot struck the first stone step, dim lights appeared at the bottom of the stairs. She pulled the shotgun up and waited several long and agonizing seconds for whatever had turned on the lights to come into sight. After several long moments, she realized that she had been holding her breath. As she let it out, more lights came on at the bottom of the staircase.

She shook her head to herself and held the gun even tighter. "I've seen this movie, and the dumb blond chick gets gutted when she investigates the strange sound at the bottom of the stairs." The sarcastic comment was concluded with her checking the load again and locking it back into place loudly. She took a deep breath and began walking slowly down the stairs.

With each step, more light shone into the narrow stairwell, which allowed her to see more and more of the walls and ceiling around her. Strange writings were arranged in a simple box method that told the reader where each story began and where its author concluded his train of thought. She passed them quickly. Her mind pulled at her to stop and investigate, but her heart took over and pushed her farther into the depths below. The path finally leveled out before her, and she walked into another large chamber. The massive expanse was vacant of anything except an enormous circular marble slab surrounded by four massive pillars that rested in the middle of the room. As Othia stepped tentatively toward it, her footsteps caused the unseen lights to grow even brighter.

The air tasted sterile, as though nothing had disturbed this chamber for hundreds, if not thousands of years. A dust-like quality lingered on everything, and as she cautiously moved forward, the off-white dust clung to her pant legs. As she surveyed the chamber, she noted that it was similar to the structure that she had discovered in Afghanistan. She turned around and saw a depiction of a man's shadow kneeling on the floor to the right of the doorway.

"I guess that is where I am supposed to stand when I start this novel." Her head slumped slightly as she noted how long it would take to decipher the messages etched on the walls in front of her. She didn't have time for this, but she could discern no other alternative.

The four pillars in the center of the room reached from the floor to the ceiling twenty feet above. They seemed to be standing sentry around the circular slab set in the middle of the subterranean chamber. She walked up alongside it and noted that the marble slab was a cover stone for something underneath. Othia traced her hands along the seam between the two pieces of stone, and her mind raced with the possibilities of what could be underneath.

Her eyes fell onto a strange marking in the middle of the cover stone. She reached over the waist-high slab and brushed the dust off the carved symbol. Etched in the stone with great care was a nearly completed triangle surrounded by the Greek symbol for omega. Her eyes began to water as she looked at the strange symbol, and her cough brought her mind back to the present. "You would think that I would remember to breathe. This isn't the first miraculous thing I have seen." She chastised herself for wasting time—precious moments that she knew her friends could not afford her to lose.

Her footsteps brought her over to the shadow on the ground, and she stared at the massive stone carvings in front of her. Each panel seemed to have a picture carved directly into the stone. The strange style of writing she had seen on the walls of the stairwell was present here as well. Without warning, the stone carvings and writing seemed to come to life. Her hands and eyes moved quickly over the tale that unfolded in front of her. These illustrations didn't have the same effect as those in Afghanistan. There was no yearning in the pit of her soul to study them, only the incessant need to complete the task at hand and help Gabriel and Samantha.

The first story was outlined with both text and carvings in incredible detail. The words swam in her vision, but her gift allowed her to make sense of them in her mind. Her newly acquired gift was working wonderfully, and she hoped it would be enough. She watched as angelic warriors flew and marched through the Gates of Heaven toward the utter blackness with banners of pure light stretched out before them. The text flooded into her mind, and a low booming voice filled her head as though she were listening to some guided tour and had finally put on her earphones.

"In the beginning, God created the heavens and the earth. As He looked at his infant creation, He wept, seeing that it was a formless void with darkness that stretched over the vast expanse of the surface of the deep. His voice rang out and created a sanctuary. Pillars of pure love and understanding stood sentry, intertwined with bars of unfailing righteousness and wrath. These protected the lavish landscape, and structures forced their way into existence at His command from the ever-encroaching darkness. The rolling hills and rich landscapes pleased him greatly, and He took great care in their construction. Time passed, and whispers passed through the walls that guarded His sanctuary.

"God strode to the gates of His new kingdom, and His eyes settled on creatures who had flourished in the darkness of the deep. His heart sank as the abominations slowly moved from the darkness into the light. Their bodies withered as they slid from the sweet embrace of the depths of the abyss into the light of their Creator. Screams of torment washed over the rolling hills of God's sanctuary as the first inhabitants of His universe saw they would never be welcome in the home of their Creator. Their deformed eyes settled on forms that walked and flew out of a haze, deep in the confines of this unattainable paradise.

"Countless beings, their bodies shining as they massed at the gates of His wondrous creation, organized into large clusters. God saw all this, and with great joy He pulled two beings to his side. One seemed to come from within Him, and the other strode from the ranks of the beings that had gathered inside the gates of His kingdom. After long moments, God turned toward his newest creations, and with his glorious finger outstretched toward the depths of the abyss, His voice thundered across the entire universe. 'Let there be light to the far ends of my creation.'

"Rhythmic beats echoed across the fabric of time and space as countless beings walked in unison out the gates of their Creator's paradise. Wars were waged in the name of the Creator across the depths of the abyss to bring the light to its farthest reaches. God turned toward the being that had come from His very bosom. 'You will command these armies of light as they bring my glory to all creation.' As a father cannot be asked to do harm to his own children, God felt He could not destroy any of His own creations personally. This caused the first angelic wars and was the fundamental beginning of the struggle of light against darkness."

Othia's eyes widened as the carvings morphed to show angelic warriors battling strange creatures, some of which seemed to be void of any shape and others that embodied every horror ever imagined. Tears welled up in her eyes as she moved to the next carving and saw the untold number of bodies that littered an empty plane of existence.

"Light was taken to every corner of creation, not only in each direction, but across every plane. Early battles were devastating and nearly wiped out one of the very legions that now protect the walls of His sanctuary. As both creations battled against one another—one fighting for survival and the other fighting by divine mandate—their tactics and savagery improved rapidly. With banners of pure light, armor of righteousness, shields of faith, and swords of spirit, the angelic armies pushed back the darkness, which unknowingly offered a new space for God's next creation."

Othia forced herself to breathe, and she sat back for a moment. Her thoughts swam as the images fought for space in her mind's eye, each deeming itself more important than the other. She focused her eyes back on the next carvings and willed her mind and body to calm down and get to the information she needed to help her friends. Out of the corner of her eye, she caught a shimmering line of text at the bottom of the carvings. The stone morphed before her again, and now massive numbers of angelic warriors were being slaughtered by the creatures of the deep.

Her eyes caught the shimmering text, and her heart leapt in her chest. "With their bodies broken, the wounded warriors of the angelic forces prayed to their Creator for help." She watched as the seriously wounded warriors seemed to heal instantly. Their wounds melted away, and the warriors simply stood and strode back into battle.

Othia stared intently at the prayers and committed them rapidly to memory. She looked around the room and saw the next wall begin to morph and change as it unveiled its story to her. She thought for a moment of the wonders she could learn, and then the mental images of Gabriel and Samantha filled her mind forcefully. "This is a big gamble, but I have to assume that it will still work if I leave and come back."

Her body ached as she rushed toward the stone stairs. Unseen lights flickered on the walls, but they did not vanish as she feared. As she crested the stairs and rushed to Samantha's side, she forced herself to pause and calm her pounding heart. Samantha's body convulsed and sprays of blood shot into the air as more fluid pooled in her collapsing lungs. Othia held her hands out over Samantha and waited until they were no longer shaking. Samantha lay unconscious below her, the dark bruises now turning yellow and green with infection. The broken bones were causing her skin to turn black as her body slowly shut itself down.

Othia began to chant softly as she knelt over Samantha's broken body. She felt her hands warm and then they pulsed with a faint white light. She slowly raised her voice and noticed that the heat and light increased. Soon her voice was bouncing off the walls as molten fire dripped from her hands onto Samantha's body. Othia's body screamed in torment. The fire spread from her hands to consume her body. Her body didn't burn, but the fire saturated her bones and stoked the fires of faith in the deepest parts of her being.

Waves of red and orange energy flowed over the length of Samantha's body. Her skin that was exposed blistered, and the edges of her clothing smoldered slightly. Othia closed her eyes tightly and continued to pray. Sounds of popping joints and bones grating together filled her ears. She forced her mind to ignore them and kept praying. She knew deep down that this was the only shot Samantha had. The fire seemed to subside on its own, and as the final waves trickled out of her hands, Othia let her face relax. She opened her eyes to see Samantha staring back at her curiously. Tears of joy and exhaustion welled in Othia's eyes.

Samantha smiled up at her. "I have been having the strangest dreams. Othia, what's wrong?"

Othia pulled Samantha up to a sitting position and then wrapped her arms around her and pulled her close. Her mind didn't want to acknowledge that this could have happened, but her heart knew the truth. The prayers had worked, and Samantha was going to be okay. Othia wept in Samantha's arms for several moments and then pulled away.

"We have to get back to the room downstairs to get help for Gabriel." The words droned off as shocked gasps escaped from Samantha's lips.

"What is wrong with him? The light that was coming off of him is gone."

"What is there now? I mean, is there anything at all?"

Samantha turned and looked at Othia. "It's kind of a dirty red. There is something there, but it seems to be fading."

Othia didn't skip a beat. She pushed herself to her feet and ran down the stone steps. Samantha didn't wait for an explanation, but hurried after her. The pair stopped at the bottom of the stairwell, and Othia simply tried to take in all the changes that had occurred in the room. Samantha was awestruck by its grandeur, and Othia was mesmerized by the stark contrast in its appearance. Othia cursed to herself. The room had changed. What had she missed? It didn't matter. The situation had demanded action, but the part of her that constantly yearned for the unknown briefly mourned the loss of such ancient information.

Othia's mind immediately noticed the additions to the chamber as they stepped onto the bottom step. The four columns still stood sentry around the cover stone in the center of the massive room. However, waves of fabric cascaded down from the ceiling, wrapping themselves around the massive columns and drawing both Othia's and Samantha's eyes to the center of the chamber. Her heart began to sink as her eyes quickly surveyed the walls of the chamber and she noticed all the murals were gone. Othia was about to scream in frustration when both women sucked in a breath as they stared at four translucent beings that carried a fifth on a wooden slab toward the cover stone. Each of the beings was dressed in armor similar to the stone guardians at the top of the stairs, but these beings seemed ancient in comparison. Their bodies shifted in and out of focus as though they were willing themselves into existence.

"Wha—" Samantha began to say, but she was cut off as Othia's hand flew over her mouth. The warning in her eyes told Samantha all she needed to know, and they sat in mute wonder as the figures approached the cover stone. A lone figure materialized at the other end of the room. It was clad in a heavy robe that hid his face from anyone in the room. The group of armored figures took slow and measured steps toward the center of the chamber and then placed the being they carried onto the marble edifice. Each of the translucent warriors moved to stand in front of the pillars that surrounded the limp body of one of their own. The

Eric Gardner

lone figure stood at the head of the marble slab and gently placed both of his hands firmly on the unmoving being's eyes and heart.

Samantha looked again at the being stretched out on the slab. Her mind pulled up the images of the two statues at the top of the stairs. She knew that she had never made it past the unnamed statue's nose, but something inside her screamed that the figure on the table was the same as the being depicted in the chamber above them. Othia's hands instinctively drew out her pad of paper and pencil. She copied all the details that her eyes could take in, not wanting to miss a single important event.

Pain flared in Samantha's ears as the being covered in robes began to speak. As she placed her hands to her ears, she could feel the warm trickle of blood run down her neck. The words were maddening to her, and she looked at Othia in wonderment as her hands worked feverishly, with no guidance from her eyes, to copy down the figure's actions and words. She couldn't understand the words the robed figure was saying, but as she watched the paper Othia was writing on, the translation became painfully clear.

"Lord of Light, our divine hammer of purity, hear our prayer. Your enemies have attacked the very soul of one of Your most devout warriors. We beseech You to cleanse his soul to allow him to fight for Your cause again."

The body on the slab began to thrash about. It contorted into all different manners of position. Bones popped, and the white fabric that draped his body was soon covered in red stains as tears in his flesh began to assault his body. Samantha looked on as the figure pulled back its hood and gazed at the other figures in the room. She watched as the lone figure addressed those that had carried in the poor wretch on the slab.

"How long has this been going on?"

One of the warriors stepped forward. "His behavior has been erratic for some time, but he fell into the sleep of the damned several suns ago. We were unsuccessful in finding a lifestream until now. Our apologies, Lord Alcon."

The lone figure's features darkened. "Your failures do not interest me. His soul has been mixed for too long. I will try and remove the taint of the firstborn, but it is unlikely that I will be successful. His death will be on your hands, and you will have to answer to the Son for your failure."

Tension built in the air as the ritual began. The figure on the table wailed in torment as the four warriors chanted in the direction of Alcon, who still stood at the head of the figure on the table. A luminous beam of white light emanated from each of the four armored beings. All four beams of light connected above the thrashing form on the slab. Brilliant white flames flowed from Alcon's hands into the eyes and heart of the tortured body that now shook violently on the stone. Something that Samantha and Othia could not see was holding the thrashing figure's legs and arms to the polished marble surface. The blood-drenched form repeatedly thrust its pelvis into the air and slammed it back onto the hardened slab. The sounds of bones and tendons breaking blended into the chanting of the warriors as cries of pain assaulted everyone in the room. Alcon lent his voice to the chorus of chants, and Samantha couldn't bring herself to look at Othia's notes to see what was being said. The screams of torment and hatred from the bloody mess on the slab filled her heart and mind with utter despair.

Time seemed to lose all meaning as the ritual went on. Samantha couldn't tell how long they had been standing there. She felt her gut twist as another set of tormented wails filled the chamber, and she looked at Othia. Her friend stood rigid. Her eyes focused on the events in the chamber, and the pencil working flawlessly to capture all the events before her. She noted that the last page was nearly full, and without skipping a beat, Othia pulled another small book from one of her pockets and continued her documentation. Red lines streaked across her eyes, and Samantha noted she was not even blinking.

As she turned to face the grisly scene again, silence fell upon the room. The light faded from the four warriors, and each looked at one another briefly. The four figures walked toward Alcon in the middle. The massive robed warrior lowered his head and shook it slowly. A defeated expression fell across his once powerful face. In unison, the four warriors drew their weapons. The light coming off the blades of their large weapons nearly blinded her, but she forced her eyes to remain fixed on the figure lying still on the slab.

Samantha jumped as in a blur of movement Alcon's massive form flew through the air and slammed into the far wall of the chamber. The loud smack was followed by a wet streaking sound as he slid down the wall, leaving a trail of bright red blood. The blood-soaked body on the slab defied its broken state and leapt up to stand defiantly against the four warriors. Samantha didn't need to look at the paper. She could hear the voice of the broken being on the slab in her head.

"This vessel is mine. Your foolish attempts at favor with the Creator shall never deny that we were first and thus favored above all. This wretch will serve us well as we take back what is rightfully ours." The echo of the creature's words filled the chamber, and Samantha watched as it turned to look each of the warriors up and down.

The popping and grating of bones caught her attention, and she squirmed as she watched the disfigured limbs shift under the saturated red cloth and change into something wholly disgusting. The once regal face twisted in pain and agony. Massive growths ballooned from beneath the skin and erupted in a torrent of pus and blood. Its limbs, once perfectly proportioned, now stretched into unnatural angles, and boils spread over all of the uncovered skin.

The four warriors stood rigid, and without warning they attacked in unison. Their blades bit sharply into the creature. Howls of pain filled the chamber again, and hatred filled the creature's eyes as it looked at each of the warriors in turn.

"Your brother doesn't understand why you are attacking us, but rest assured that I have told him the truth about your kind. His will is strong, but I will keep him in the depths of my soul where even his memories will become polluted and his soul will wither in agony for all eternity."

The four attacked again, but the creature leapt free of the table, taking one of the warriors by surprise. There was a clamor of armor hitting the floor and then a sucking sound as the head of the warrior rolled across the unblemished floor. As their companion fell, the warriors rushed into action, attacking with all their might the thing that was now responsible for three deaths in its new form.

A flurry of attacks from two sides were a blur to Samantha, and she only understood the outcome when two of the warriors fell as their own weapons were used against them. Their bodies collapsed in heaping masses of flesh and armor. The last warrior squared off with the creature. His sword pulsed with light as he watched the creature pace before him.

"Your friends are tasty, little one, but your death will be the sweetest, because it will mark my freedom." The creature lunged at the warrior with gore-covered clawed hands stretched out before it. In a flurry of motion, the lone warrior rolled under the creature, and his weapon arched up and drove through the creature's chest. The momentum sent them crashing to the floor. The creature looked down at the warrior and screamed in defiance. Rotting flesh and spit dripped from its mouth.

The warrior grunted with effort as he stood. The creature was impaled on the end of his sword, and the blade's light flowed into the vile being. He stood for a moment. His helmet masked his facial features, but the hatred that emanated from his body filled the air. With one fluid motion, he lifted the creature on his blade and slammed its broken frame onto the marble slab. The mutated body split into two pieces and burst into black flames. Cries of anguish and defeat washed over the room, and for several moments the flames consumed the creature's remains.

Samantha watched as the beings began to fade. She looked at the warrior now standing in the middle of the room, and she locked her eyes on his helmet. As the warrior removed the beautiful armor from his head, her jaw went slack. Her mind instantly remembered the rugged features, the hard eyes, and the inspiring prowess. He was the statue at the top of the stairs. This was the angel Othia had called Abaddon.

Chapter 19
Always Read the Fine Print

If it seems too good to be true, it probably is.
~ Good advice

Location: Unknown

Othia and Samantha both stood on either end of Gabriel's still body. His breathing was becoming more erratic, and his face was turning the color of ash. They both knew what was happening after seeing the horrific events below.

"What do we do? I mean, is it safe to move him? And what happens if he changes like that thing downstairs?"

Othia shook her head. "I don't know, but we need to do something fast or he won't have any chance at all. Alcon said that the others had taken too much time, and it had complicated the ritual." She flipped through the pages of her book and reviewed what was written.

Samantha held back from telling Othia about her ability to write without glancing at the pages and how it had deeply unnerved her. They needed to help Gabriel, and conversations like that would have to wait for later.

"Come on, Samantha, you grab his legs, and I'll get his shoulders." With grunts of effort accompanied by several painful falls, they descended the stairs and arrived at the cover stone in the lower chamber. Othia glanced around and saw that everything looked the same as the last time they had arrived at the base of the stairs. They struggled, each of them on the verge of exhaustion, as they did their best to place Gabriel softly onto the ground.

"He is going to have one hell of a headache after some of those falls on the way down."

Othia barely heard the comment from Samantha as she flipped through her book again to ensure they were doing everything right.

Samantha looked around the room. Chills ran up and down her spine as she recalled the fight that had happened only moments ago. There was no sign anywhere that a struggle had taken place. The hulking angelic warriors had vanished as though they had been a dream. She turned as Othia let out a strained grunt behind her. She had placed Gabriel on the table as gently as she could and then looked over at Samantha.

"I didn't want to disturb you. I know how unnerving this chamber can be."

Samantha nodded her head in appreciation and then moved to help out however she could with Gabriel. The women moved to the pillars where they had seen the four warriors stand.

Othia had thought about standing where she had seen Alcon leading the ritual, but something just felt wrong with it. She handed Samantha the shotgun from her waistband. "There are two slugs loaded. Remember to aim lower than normal, because people tend to shoot high when they get nervous."

Samantha nodded. "How will I know if I need to use it?"

"Wait for him to change like that thing we saw earlier. If that happens, it won't be Gabriel anymore, and killing it will be okay." Othia saw the terror in Samantha's face, but there was nothing that either of them could do. This had to be done, and it needed to happen now or they risked never being able to help their possessed friend.

Othia read from her notes, concentrating and struggling to get each word perfectly right, and Samantha marveled at how much her voice sounded like the ceremony they had watched earlier. The words whirled around the room, almost blending into one another. A warming sensation began to build in Othia's throat, as it had in her hands with Samantha, and her heart leapt. She cursed at herself mentally for getting distracted, and focused on the words again.

The room swam with the strange words as they blended together. Samantha had to cover her ears. The words had the same effect on her as the teacups at the amusement park. Her vision began to spin, so she focused her eyes on the floor in an attempt to stay on her feet. Grabbing the wall didn't seem to help, and she hoped that the floor would stay put too, at least until Othia was finished. The room continued to spin as Othia's voice reached a climactic boom, and the echoes of her words swirled around, saturating everything around them.

As the sound faded, Samantha looked up. The incapacitating noise now faded and with it the dizziness. The two women stared for what seemed like an eternity, waiting for some sign of life from Gabriel's still form on the slab.

Othia let out a startled cry when Gabriel's back arched and an animalistic roar left his lips. His body slammed back onto the cover stone, and a black mist exploded from his mouth and nose. It shot toward the ceiling, but just before coming into contact with the mosaics of the angelic warriors, the mist fell to the floor around the cover stone where Gabriel lay. Othia and Samantha watched as the black mist crept back up the smooth stone that supported the covering slab and slid into the seam where the two massive pieces met. It was gone in a few heartbeats, and Othia then heard, rather than saw, the first signs of life from her friend.

Gabriel moved gingerly on the slab. His eyes blinked as they tried to get accustomed to the light. He slowly sat up. "What is going on? I have been having some really crazy dreams."

Both Othia and Samantha ran to him and hugged his sweaty form before Othia pulled back. "How do you feel?"

Gabriel looked at her for a moment and then shook his head. "Cold, like I have been sitting in the snow with nothing on. And I have a monster of a headache. How did I get here, guys?"

"It's a long story, and we need to do other things first. Let's get you off this thing and back onto your feet."

The trio froze when Gabriel's feet struck the ground. There was a soft murmur in the floor and then the room began to shift before them. The pillars sank into the floor, and the walls began to take the shape of the murals again. The cover stone remained intact, and as the trio watched, the room morphed itself back to the initial configuration that Othia had seen.

"Really, guys, what in the hell is going on here?"

Othia looked at Samantha and each of them nodded.

The small amount of color that had returned back to Gabriel's face left rapidly as he listened to the recap of the events. Othia stopped several times to make sure he was okay, and Samantha kept encouraging him to eat or drink something. When they were done, Gabriel sat speechless for several moments.

"I would say let me process this, but I don't think we have that kind of time. What now?"

Othia shook her head. "I have to see what is new in here. The last time I needed information the chamber gave it freely. Each time it knew what I was looking for, and the walls told me, or at least let me see, whatever it could offer for help. I don't know what this place is, but so far we have been getting some solid answers when we have gone looking."

Samantha helped Gabriel up while Othia moved to the area to the right of the stairs. There she found the same outline of a man on the ground, similar to the shadow that she had seen when looking for answers for Samantha's injuries, but the murals had changed. They were now strikingly similar to those she had seen in Afghanistan.

The murals on the walls were made from the same precious material, and all the walls were different from what she had seen before. The murals didn't move like the stone works had hours earlier, but the portrayal of the information was still as striking as ever. The first was simplistic in nature: it showed a very large group of beings standing on one side of a body of water and a black blob to their right, and then on the other side was another group of the same number of beings with the blob on their left. The black mass was beyond anything she had seen before. It didn't hold any true shape, but when she looked closely between both depictions the shapes was the same. Even though the black mass was an undistinguishable shape, it was depicted precisely in both of the mosaics. She took some notes and then moved to the second mural.

This was a more elaborate telling of the same story. This one looked similar to the chamber they found themselves in now. There was a black blob in the middle where the cover stone was, but there were strange beings standing in the shadow of the mural. As her fingers traced the path of the story, it came to life in her mind.

"The cover stone had been removed, or unblocked, causing something to happen. Something that allowed a group to move from one place to another without actually crossing the area. The blackness is the key in all the murals." She spoke to herself, but Gabriel and Samantha had moved in behind her and listened intently as she deciphered the ancient pictures. The figures in the darkness intrigued her. They seemed to be assuming the position of ancient prayer. As she moved to the next scene, she saw that they were praying and as they did the blackness got smaller. By the end of the mural, the blackness had dissipated, and the figures were leaving the chamber.

She walked to the next mural and paused. She was sure it was an image of the same chamber they stood in. The engravings were identical to those on top of the cover stone, and the layout was the same. The blackness was there, but there were no figures in the shadow. Strange beasts were shown coming out of the black mass, and she saw the same warriors she had seen in Afghanistan battling these beasts. Ultimately, the warriors erased the blackness and brought normality to the chamber.

Othia quickly looked at the other murals in the room and then rejoined Gabriel and Samantha. "They are all the same, more or less. I think we can get out of here, but I don't know whether we really want to."

Samantha and Gabriel looked quizzically at each other and then back at Othia. She raised a hand and hurriedly told them her thought process, "This thing in the middle of the room can cause a kind of blackness to appear, allowing people or things to move from one area to another, regardless of any obstacle or distance. I know how to open it, but the murals warn that the blackness must be made to disappear, or creatures from inside the blackness will come out. It says that it can be closed with the true words of God or a sacrifice of flesh."

She looked at the faces of Gabriel and Samantha and noted that Gabriel was trying to understand, but that Samantha was moving ahead of him. "What is your take on this, Samantha? You look as though you have it figured out."

Samantha looked at Othia for a moment, collecting her thoughts, and then smiled. "I studied this in school. Modern science is working on this stuff right now. Scientists theorize on what the murals are talking about; they call it a wormhole. Science-fiction movies, shows, and books are always taking it to the extreme, but that is essentially what this is. It is basically bending or ripping time and space as we know it. When you go into point A to get to point B, you're really not traveling any distance, but merely creating a hole in time and space so that you can step from one place to the other. No research that I know of has even gone further than theory right now, and of course, I have never heard of things coming through." Samantha was beaming from ear to ear, her confidence building at finally being able to contribute something solid to the group.

Gabriel shook his head. "I have watched my fair share of movies and TV, and I have never heard of prayers doing anything but giving television evangelists the power to drain your wallet."

"The true word of God is what brought you back and healed Samantha. I know it sounds strange, but I don't think it's really a matter of *how* it works but really a matter of *should* we do it or not?"

"What do you mean?"

The three sat down on the floor, and Othia leaned against one of the walls. "Each of these murals, except for the first one, showed some sort of sacrifice going on. The word of God is used in some; others show a body lying at the base of the hole. No... that's not right. I think what you said before, Samantha, is correct: it's a rip. Whatever power is in the prayer around the cover stone rips open time and space to let us pass from one point to another, which, by the way, is the only way I think we are going to get out of here. We go in one area and come out another."

"How do we know where it is going to take us?" Gabriel looked at Othia expectantly.

She shook her head. "It doesn't give any real specifics. It could take us anywhere, but anywhere has to be better than this, right? We are just about out of food, and we used up the last of the water ten minutes ago. But like I said, the part that worries me is the sacrifice. One of us would have to stay behind so that we could recite the words to allow the rip to close. After all, I don't think the alternative is a very good idea."

They all nodded and sat for a while, each of them mulling over the problem and trying to find a viable solution. Gabriel was the first to stand and walk back toward the stairs.

"Where are you going, Gabriel?" Othia was about to stand when he held up a hand to stop her.

"I think I know where our sacrifice is going to come from. Wait here." Gabriel bounded up the steps, and he could hear Othia and Samantha talking to one another and trying to guess what he was doing. He crested the landing and looked over to the far corner of the entryway. There, still smoldering and rotting, were the remains of the creature that had tried to attack him and do who knows what with his mind and body. He took off his shirt and wrapped up as much of the rotting gray mass as he could carry. The putrid smell of vomit and feces wafted up to his nose, and he turned rapidly away. His shirt held as much as he dared to pick up, and he walked gingerly back down the stairs. There was really nothing left of the creature, but Gabriel hoped it was enough to facilitate the sacrifice. Appeasing *what*, he didn't know.

As he came into view of Samantha and Othia, he saw their shocked faces and watched Samantha pull the shotgun level, tentatively aiming it at him. "I am fine, really. Here is what I think we should use. After all, it doesn't say that the sacrifice has to be living, right? This thing still feels evil, so maybe it still has some juice in it to count for something."

The women shared a look of uneasiness, but nodded as Gabriel placed the remains at the base of the marble slab. Othia looked over her notes one last time and then closed her book and placed it in her satchel.

"Othia, do you want us to help while you are doing... well, whatever it is you are going to do?"

Othia shook her head as Gabriel looked from one woman to the other. "No, just stand there and watch. I don't know what this is going to do, but be ready to run or shoot if anything comes out of the darkness—and pray this works. I have been all over these two chambers, and there is no way in or out except this. I can only hope we are doing the right thing."

Gabriel and Samantha both nodded and moved a little farther from the slab in the middle of the room. Samantha passed the shotgun back to Gabriel and felt the burden of what it had represented gratefully leave her body.

Othia began to chant, and her voice gained momentum as she uttered the words from her memory out loud in the chamber. As her voice grew louder, Gabriel and Samantha felt a strange tingle in their limbs that grew in intensity as Othia's voice became louder and louder, until she was shouting at the top of her lungs. Gabriel couldn't tell what amplified her voice so loud and then his thoughts swept away as he and Samantha were struck with a gale-force wind that nearly knocked them to the ground.

Gabriel reached out quickly and caught Samantha. The two used each other for balance and looked into the wind in an attempt to discern where it was coming from. The intensity continued to build as Othia shouted the strange language into the air. The ground began to shake, and the solid stone floor quivered as the next stage of the ritual commenced. Both Gabriel and Samantha were thrown against the closest wall. The wind knocked out of them, and each fought to get off the ground to be ready for whatever might come next. As the room shook and swayed, the wind whipped past Gabriel, and he saw that Othia was standing perfectly still, as if in the eye of whatever strange storm was brewing.

Pain shot into his ears as a million childlike voices cried out in one voice. Terror-stricken and saturated with pain, the voices bounced around the chamber, fading in and out as if being tuned in. Samantha put her hands over her ears and felt a familiar warm stickiness. As she pulled her hands away, she saw them again covered in blood. Fear crept into her eyes as she looked over at Gabriel and noticed that his ears were bleeding as well. Her eyes followed his as he stared at the center of the room, and the fevered pitch of the cries of pain continued to climb. Both watched in mute fascination as a small black circle abruptly came into existence. It grew as the cries of pain escalated, each apparently feeding off the other. Othia's voice was all but drowned out as the cries and wind circled the room. Gabriel watched as her mouth moved, and her expression showed that she was still straining to have her voice heard.

As the blackness grew, its shape changed and began to look like the depictions on the wall. There was a jaggedness about the thing; it truly looked as though they had ripped something apart. A memory flooded back into Gabriel's head of the demon that had attacked them earlier. Terror gripped his heart, and he grabbed Samantha and pulled her toward Othia, intent on stopping this ritual before anything could come through. How had they forgotten that the creature had come out of a similar hole? He knew there was no place for them to hide, and if that creature attacked again, there would be nothing left of them.

He pulled Samantha behind him and fought to move toward Othia. His steps began to falter and then the wind and the violent rocking of the room stopped as suddenly as they had started. Othia's voice was now a whisper in the chamber, and the cries of the unseen children faded as well. There was now a jagged black shape suspended four feet above the ground and stretching seven feet into the air. It looked as though it could fit one person at a time, and the blackness seemed to move with their line of sight. Gabriel looked over at Othia and saw her swaying dangerously back and forth. He rushed to catch her before she fell to the floor.

As he eased her down, she looked up at him and then over to Samantha. "We have to hurry. There are only a few minutes that it will stay open since we are not staying to close it. Look at the slab. I guess they took your gift after all, Gabriel." All three looked at the marble slab where Gabriel had placed the remains of the creature that had attacked them. All that remained was a wet stain where they had been resting only moments ago.

Samantha and Gabriel helped Othia to her feet and then the three moved toward the gaping hole. Gabriel looked at each of them. "Well, since I have the gun, I'll go first. If there is anything on the other side, I will try to hold it off until you both get there." Samantha and Othia didn't object. They all quickly picked up their meager belongings and stood close together. "Do you think this stuff will make it through with us?"

Othia nodded her head. "It says that anything can move through the rip. At least, that is what the wall says."

"Okay, here we go. If you hear shooting when you exit, hit the ground and find cover. Othia, you're second in, and Samantha, you pull up the rear and make sure Othia makes it in, okay?" Samantha nodded, and the three fell in line.

Gabriel walked slowly toward the blackness. He noticed that his hands and feet were sweating. He laughed at himself. Why shouldn't they be? This wasn't exactly the most normal thing he had ever done. As he edged closer to the shimmering blackness before him, he felt a frigid chill on his face. It wasn't a breeze, but like dry ice was being stuck to his skin.

He swallowed hard and straightened his shoulders. "For my family," he whispered as he took one final step into the unknown.

Othia and Samantha watched him simply walk into the darkness, and then he was gone. They both looked at one another and then Othia took a step toward the unknown. Samantha grabbed her shoulder, and she froze in her tracks.

"What if we die doing this? What if wherever we are going is worse than here?"

Othia didn't turn around but simply patted her hand and shook her head. "If it is worse than what we have already gone through, it will be a short trip and a really long vacation when we get to Heaven. Follow me. And if we don't make it, I will walk through the gates with you." Othia felt her grip give a little and then walked briskly into the blackness.

Samantha stood alone for the first time in what seemed like an eternity. She stared into the blackness and saw it shimmer, almost like it was fading. Her heart skipped a beat, and while the fear of the unknown still lingered in her heart, the fear of being alone propelled her into the darkness—and then her world spun out of control.

Books of the Thirteenth Legion Series
Book 1- Defiance

Book 2- Awakening

Book 3- Sacrifice

Eric Gardner

Book 4- Gathering

(Spring 2017)

Made in the USA
Columbia, SC
20 June 2017